SECOND CHANCE
Sister

Linda Kepner

CRIMSON
ROMANCE
F+W Media, Inc.

This edition published by
Crimson Romance
an imprint of F+W Media, Inc.
10151 Carver Road, Suite 200
Blue Ash, Ohio 45242

www.crimsonromance.com

ISBN 10: 1-4405-6257-1
ISBN 13: 978-1-4405-6257-0
eISBN 10: 1-4405-6258-X
eISBN 13: 978-1-4405-6258-7

Acknowledgments

The author wishes to thank the NH Chapter of the Romance Writers Association for encouragement, good-fellowship, and support. Many thanks also to editor Jennifer Lawler and the talented staff of Crimson Romance Publishing, and also the Ladies In Red, the network of Crimson Romance authors.

Information about Ile de la Reunion is derived mainly from the Internet, French school sites, and tour books, with some back-dating to 1969. Much of Bishou's academic knowledge and experience is derived from my own experiences at Keene State College and the unique World Studies program of Eisenhower College.

CHAPTER 1

Paradise, thought Bishou Howard, as Louis drove the little Mercedes through the tropical jungle roads of Réunion Island. Like any *réunionnais* duo, they had spent their day picnicking. And talking. Bishou smiled and thought, *a loaf of bread, a jug of wine, and thou by my side.*

Everyone always drove slowly out here. Louis's dark eyes glanced away from the grassy road—there was no danger of a crash at this speed—and he inquired, "Did hearing me say that I love you as much as I love this island make you smile like that?"

Why lie? "Yes."

Louis laughed. *I've never heard him laugh like this*, Bishou thought. *He really is happy.*

They drove back into Saint-Denis. Bishou realized with surprise that Louis had driven onto Rue Marché, Market Street, and had, in fact, pulled up in front of the jewelers. She was half-asleep, and had not paid attention to directions.

"Louis, this is not the pension," she protested.

"I know. But we have other things we must do," he replied. "*Viens.*" Come. Wordlessly, she accompanied him into the jewelry store.

It was late in the day, almost sunset, but the stores here stayed open longer because of the early-afternoon siesta. The store manager, an elegant polished Frenchman, almost wrung his hands with delight when he saw his customers. "Why, Monsieur Dessant, welcome! What may we do for you today?"

"Bonjour, Monsieur Charron," said Louis. "We had discussed a necklace?"

Necklace? She blinked. Monsieur Charron, however, understood at once.

"I inquired, Monsieur. It is more an American custom than a French one, but I was able to order what you wanted." From a display case, he removed a piece, and set it on the counter.

Bishou stared. Strung upon a short gold chain was an inch-long gold-and-diamond pendant, showing three stripes—the chevrons of a doctoral gown. "Louis," she said softly, stunned. A doctoral charm, to celebrate the fact that she was the third-ever female to earn a Ph.D. at East Virginia University! She turned the charm over, and saw the tiny "8/16/69," the date written American-style, commemorating that victory, a little over a month ago.

Louis smiled, very pleased. "Let us see how it looks, shall we?" The jeweler detached it from its stand and gave it to Louis. Bishou stood still while he fastened it around her neck. She stared at her reflection in the mirror the jeweler held before her. Louis murmured in her ear, "It looks quite right."

"Louis."

"Now for the rings."

Bishou shook her head and tried to chase away the numbness. "I am not—I don't think I am quite the kind of woman...I mean, diamonds."

"I thought of that. Also, the ring you gave me Thursday night, your college ring, has a blue stone. How do you feel about sapphires?"

"I—" She gathered her thoughts. "Whatever you want, *mon mari*." My husband. The first time she called him that. She saw the warmth in his smile.

The rest of the visit was a blur. The men found a solitary sapphire, in a white-gold band, and fitted it to her finger. The manager sized them for wedding bands, and came up with simple bands that matched the engagement ring. These he placed in a box, which Louis tucked away in his pocket. The bands were not engraved; that could wait for another day. Weddings took place quickly on Réunion Island, Louis had told her. They were dawdling by réunionnais standards. She had said yes the night before last, Thursday night, and they would be married in eight days, on Friday. If they could overcome some formidable obstacles between now and then.

The men transacted their business while she waited, silent and numb. Then Louis smilingly escorted her out of the shop, and back into the little white car. He got in, and put an arm around her shoulder. He saw that she still looked numb, chuckled, and kissed her. "What color is the stone of your ring?" he challenged her.

In English, Bishou replied, "True blue."

His face grew suddenly serious. Then Louis replied, "Yes, true blue," and kissed her again.

*

Louis helped Bishou gather all her packages out of the trunk when they reached the pension. "Remember, church, nine o'clock. I will pick you up at a quarter to nine," Louis said.

"I will remember," she promised. "And thank you."

He opened the pension door for her, kissed her despite her arms full of packages, and drew the door shut behind her. She heard the engine start as he drove away.

Eliane, the elder of the two sisters who ran the Pension Étoile, smiled at her armload. Joseph, their Creole porter, came forward, grinning, and relieved her of some of her burden. "Well, mademoiselle! You have certainly been busy with your refund," Eliane teased.

"I have so much to do, and so little time in which to do it," said Bishou.

"Certainly, certainly." Eliane sounded as excited as she was. "I had meant to ask before—do you plan to be married here, out of the pension?"

"Do you mean—where I get dressed before the ceremony, and so on?" At Eliane's nod, Bishou replied, "I presume so. I'm hoping these things all fall together as we get closer."

"Is it a church wedding?"

"Well," Bishou replied, "that is tomorrow's problem." She and Joseph made their way up the stairs.

She rummaged around her purse for a tip for Joseph, and said, "Thank you for all your help, *mon ami*. I think you mentioned me to your friends and family, too, and they have helped me as well."

"Ah," said Joseph, pocketing the handful of coins she gave him, "we are all *réunionnaises* together."

"*Bien dit*. But I am *étrangère* and grateful for your assistance."

The kindly Creole smiled, touched his cap, and left.

Bishou closed the door, unbagged things, and hung up clothes on her few available hangers. She slipped on the elegant shoes Louis purchased for some walking practice around the room. She slid out her Sunday hat, a little headpiece with netting attached, and fluffed it out; it had got squished in the backpack. Her white print dress would do for church. She ought to have gloves, and white sandals. Ah, well. Later.

Bishou sat on the bed, pulled out her portfolio, and began an outline of her expository lecture for Wednesday. Wednesday problems first, Friday problems later. Still full of bread and cheese and wine, Bishou decided to forego supper.

She was beginning to doze off when she heard a tap-tap at the door. "*Entrez!*"

Marie, Eliane's younger sister and co-hostess, peeped in. "Mademoiselle. Ah, what beautiful shoes!"

Bishou smiled and stood up. "They are not my style, but Louis likes them. What do you think?"

"They're lovely! We're having a little evening meal, downstairs.

Come. Eliane said you looked so tired, I knew you wouldn't get yourself something to eat. Come," Marie persuaded. Bishou allowed herself to be herded downstairs, into their little living quarters at the back.

Of course she showed them the engagement ring. They oohed and aahed over it, even though it was the doctorate charm that meant so much more to Bishou.

"I wondered," said Eliane, in a tentative tone of voice, "if there might be some problem with Monsieur Dessant being married in a church."

"I don't know, either," Bishou admitted. "He is going to ask tomorrow."

"Well, we will be at the nine o'clock Mass as well," said Eliane decisively, "and we will pray for the best for you."

"Thank you. You are kind. I so want him to be happy."

"There speaks an old-fashioned woman," said Marie, surprised. "I thought you were one of these 'new' women, *mademoiselle*, with your college professorship and all!"

"I have a right to choose some of both worlds, don't I?" Bishou asked. "Isn't that what this 'women's liberation' is all about?"

"Well, of course, Bishou, but not to break your back under the additional burden."

"Well, then, you had best pray for me, too."

*

Bishou woke up in plenty of time to dress for church. She came downstairs to an empty lobby, and realized the ladies were dressing, too. There would be no breakfast until they returned from communion. Bishou slipped out the front door, and waited for Louis.

He pulled up promptly at a quarter to nine. He opened the door for her, then returned to his seat. "*Très jolie*. I like that little hat."

"*Merci.*"

He pulled out and drove to Église de Saint-Denis, a beautiful stone-and-stucco Catholic church in another part of the city. It had spacious grounds: a side yard, a vestry, a short wall around it. Louis parked, as was his custom, and they joined others entering the church just as the bells pealed. They blessed themselves, and took a side aisle seat halfway back. As Louis knelt to pray, Bishou kept him company, and took a seat as he did.

Bishou remained silent but observant. The white French population tended toward the front of the church, the dark Creole population to the rear. They were, so to speak, at the rear of the church. It was a fairly large church, and well-populated. But Louis spoke to no one, and kept to himself. There were only one or two people in nearby pews, strangers.

The procession and music were familiar to her. The procession passed down their side aisle, and up the center. Bishou thought the priest, a Creole, glanced at them, but she might have imagined it. The Mass progressed like all Masses had done for centuries. There was silence between herself and Louis. Père Reynaud had a very gentle voice, although she could hear him well enough. His sermon was merely an expository on this week's gospel, not particularly inspiring. She did not take communion because Louis did not. After the recessional, she waited for Louis to leave. However, he remained in his seat.

When the church was almost empty, Louis stood. "Wait here," he told her, and left for the front, in the direction the Père had gone.

She sat and waited, letting the quiet of the empty church soak in. In a little while, she heard footsteps. Both Louis and the Père were there. Bishou stood.

"Father, permit me to introduce my fiancée, Bishou Howard."

"*Bonjour*, my daughter, and welcome." The priest looked a little surprised; apparently, Louis was dropping a brick on him.

"*Bonjour*, Father," she said, and no more.

"You see why I wished to speak to you, Père," said Louis. "I need to know if I can be married, Friday, in this church—or not."

"I see." The priest sat down in the pew behind her, with Louis. She sat again and twisted to face them. "My daughter, are you a Catholic?"

"Oui, père."

"Where were you baptized?"

"Église de Sacré-Coeur, Montreal, Quebec."

"And your home parish now?"

"Église de Saint-Patrick, Boston, Massachusetts."

The priest permitted himself a small smile. "I gather you have no intent to be married in your home parish."

She matched his tiny smile. "Non, Père."

There was a long silence. Pere Reynaud sighed. "This is a serious problem, Monsieur Dessant."

"I know, Père," said Louis.

Bishou took a breath to speak. Louis saw, held up his hand, and she let the breath out again.

The priest continued to sit there in silence, frowning in thought. At last, he said, "It is a long and hard road if you so choose it, Monsieur Dessant, a road back to the faith."

Again, Bishou moved to speak. Again, Louis held up a hand. This time, she said, "Non, Louis, I will not hold my tongue. Père, why do you call him Monsieur Dessant? Is he not Louis? Is he not also one of your children?"

"Bishou." Louis held up a hand. His voice was firm. "*Silence, ma chère.*"

"*Oui, mon cher. Mes apologies, Père.*" She turned away from them, and faced front.

After another moment of thought, Père Reynaud said, "Come into the sacristy with me, Louis."

"Oui, Père."

The men's footsteps echoed in the empty church as they walked to the front, where the Père opened the door from which the procession had emerged. There was light within. In a moment, in the rectangle of light from that doorway, she saw Louis kneel on a prie-dieu and clasp his hands. The Père was not in her view, but she could see Louis's bowed head, and saw his lips move as he answered questions. The voices themselves were the indistinguishable murmurs of two men.

Louis kept his hands folded as he answered questions, but she saw more animation in his replies as they became lengthier. She wondered if he and the Père had spoken at all since the day of Louis' first wedding, the marriage that had evolved into deceit and disaster—Louis' false bride, his headlong descent into a life of crime. Louis bowed his head, as if accepting a blessing. Then he took a packet from the priest and stood. Together, they came into the church again.

She knew her anxiety was in her eyes, but she didn't bother to disguise it.

Père Reynaud bent over her and said with a smile, "We'll see you on Friday, then."

Bishou burst into tears.

Louis didn't look very surprised as he half-lifted her to her feet. "Why, my formidable *Americaine*! I was not sure you even knew how to weep."

"This was so important," she sobbed.

Louis gathered her into his arms. "*Mon tresor,*" he said, sounding close to tears himself, "we are all right. Sh, sh." To the priest, he said, "Friday morning, then, nine o'clock. *Au revoir, Père.*"

"*Au revoir, mes enfants,*" said Père Reynaud, and he was smiling. He signed a cross over their heads, turned, and left again for the sacristy as they made their way outside.

Beside the car, Louis fished out his handkerchief. "*Cherie,* don't cry, please."

"Hard to—to stop, once I start," she sobbed. "I'm sorry. I was trying so hard."

He wiped her face. "And you defended me, *ma tigresse*."

"You laugh at me."

"Non, non," he protested softly, still wiping away tears. "Or if I do, it is because you made Père Reynaud laugh, too. This time, he understands that I marry for love." He maneuvered her into the car, and got in himself. "I know what we will do. There is a little fisherman's café down the coast road, toward Saint-Benoit. I know you like your seafood, *hein*? We will see what the catch of the day is."

"I like that idea." Bishou smiled through her tears.

"*Bon*, then that is what we will do."

*

The little fishermen's café had mussels today, and they were wonderful, accompanied by white wine and good bread and butter. They sat inside, the easier for Bishou's red-rimmed eyes. Louis told her what had happened. "My first confession...since before my first wedding. Then he asked about my time in France, prison and all. And then...about you. I said many things I am glad you could not hear." Louis sipped the wine. "Good things, I assure you, but I might have made you blush. And he asked about my hopes and dreams. I have never had a priest ask that." There was another pause while he freed a mussel from its shell. "I think I have you to thank for that, *ma cherie*."

"I am headstrong. I'm sorry I disobeyed you."

"Pfah." Louis shook his head. "You did right. When he called me Louis, in your hearing—I think that was the first time he ever called me Louis. I think you made him realize he was treating Frenchmen, *zoreils*, different from native Creoles."

"Did he say so?"

"*Non*. And I would not have been rude enough to ask if he had a higher standard for me than he did for some *apache* off the street." There was a twinkle in his eye. "But I did notice that those instructions he gave me for my indulgence were already made up in packets."

"Is this something that must be completed before the wedding?"

"*Non, non*. He takes my word on this. Well, God is overseeing us all, I had best keep that word, *hein?*" Another mussel. "Rosary time every night until further notice, prayers from the little booklet he gave me; I think I am making up in one bundle all the prayer I have skipped for ten years." He reached out, and clasped her hand for a moment. "But it is in a good cause."

"I am sorry to be more upset than you are."

"Pfah." He shook his head again, and operated on another mussel. "You do not know what peace I felt this morning, with you beside me, in the church. As long as you are with me, *ma Bishou*, this is a very agreeable penance."

"Oh, surely, since I am the one who got upset."

Louis chuckled and ate another bite. "Your turn today, mine tomorrow." That was an old gamblers' saying, worthy of the tobacco auctions. "You are not yet sorry you said yes to me, are you? Do you now have the cold feet?"

"No, I am committed."

He laughed and almost choked on his wine. "Yes, baby, you are committed. If you were to say, 'Oh, no, Louis, it was all my mistake' to me now, I would fling you over my shoulder and carry you to the church Friday."

"You just try it, that's all," Bishou told him. Her own appetite was recovering. "Now my only remaining battle is the dress I will wear." She thought of Madame Nadine, the elegant local dressmaker, snarling, "I am not a dressmaker to American working girls, or rich Americans, nor will I be. The women of France and Reunion Island, these are for whom I make my fashions."

"If all else fails, wear this outfit. It's nice." He pointed toward what she wore, although the hat was now out in the car. "With the new little shoes."

"*Oui*, with the new little shoes," she said with a smile.

"Madame Nadine snorts that she will only serve *réunionnaises*, very well, you are becoming one. If she will not serve you, *tant pis*. There are plenty of other dressmakers throughout the world." He spoke with the easy confidence of a millionaire.

"What was she talking to you about?" Bishou wanted to know. When the dressmaker stood with Louis outside the shoe store, he had very evidently appeared to wish to be somewhere else.

"Oh." He reddened. "She did not know why I was waiting in the street, of course, so she came to pass the time of day with me. She is very intense. I think she would have—how did you say it—would have thrown me over her saddle and carried me off to rescue me, if she could."

Bishou smiled and leaned back in her seat. "Oh, then I was correct in that impression." Now she had another question. "Louis—*am* I rescuing you?"

Louis glanced at her. "Perhaps a little. But you know, it is not one-sided. You are not flinging me over your saddle. I am climbing up on the horse, pulling you up behind me and saying, 'Oh please, Bishou, rescue me.'"

She chuckled at the grain of truth. "As long as we know where we stand."

"*Oui*." He reached out and clasped her hand again. "I have committed terrible crimes, Bishou. I know that."

"You *didn't* know, Louis. How could you have known that the woman who came to marry you had killed another woman and taken her place?"

"I know." Louis sighed and frowned. "But you know, Celie's sister, Adrienne, was adamant that I remain in prison, that I could never be forgiven for losing my heart to the wrong woman.

Mon agent de liberation conditionnelle—I don't know the English term—"

"Parole officer."

"*Oui*, parole officer—still receives letters from Adrienne, saying I have not been punished nearly enough for my sins." A cloud passed over Louis's expressive features. "From her point of view, that might be the truth. I did not murder Celie Bourjois, but I was a willing accessory."

"Who spent seven years at hard labor to atone for it." Bishou rested her hand upon his. "Louis, if Père Reynaud—and God—can find it in their hearts to forgive you, what more do you need?"

The cloud passed. Louis smiled and patted her hand, reassured. The manageress came over, and he paid their bill. Full of wine and mussels, they began their return journey, turning inland a bit. Louis took jungle roads he knew, and Bishou just enjoyed the ride. A riot of colors met her eyes. Once, in the far distance, she saw le Piton de la Fournaise, the volcano that had created the island.

Chapter 2

They were almost home, driving along the road toward the cigarette factory, when Louis pulled over suddenly and abruptly to the roadside, yanked on the parking brake, and shut off the engine. He grabbed something from the door pocket, jumped out, and ran across a field where other men were working. In surprise, followed by alarm, Bishou realized he was carrying a machete. A second thought occurred to her—this was Sunday, the men shouldn't be working. She saw them, half a field away, chopping, and thought: *Tobacco rust. Pruning with the machete.* Just as they had discussed at that workshop at East Virginia University, months ago, when she first met Louis Dessant.

Louis was talking to a Creole, evidently a foreman, and took a few chops himself at a tobacco plant, lifted the leaves, and examined them. Machetes in hand, he and the foreman walked further back in the field and were lost to her sight. She waited patiently. This was a business crisis.

Fifteen or twenty minutes passed before she saw them walking back toward the car. The foreman didn't look worried; neither did Louis. Louis, however, looked determined. They walked right up to her car door.

"Bishou, this is François Dellerand, my field foreman," Louis introduced her. "François, *ma fiancée* Bishou."

"*Bonjour*, mam'selle."

"*Bonjour*, monsieur," she replied courteously.

Louis paid little attention to the amenities. "You don't know how to send transoceanic cables, do you?"

"Non, I don't."

"Can you drive this *voiture?*" he asked, equally intently.

17

"Yes," she admitted. She always let him drive. As her brother Jean-Baptiste (Bat) often said, *Driving is a man thing.*

"Have you got paper and pencil in your purse?" Bishou pulled them out. Louis wrote an address, then a name she recognized as an antibiotic. "You will go into Saint-Denis. This street is a right turn off Rue Marché, a few blocks before you reach the retail district. This is the address for Claire Aucoeur's flat—she's on the second floor. You will take her to the factory and she will send a cable to the Sorbonne, that we need this drug to Garros Airport by the first plane tomorrow morning, details please telephone us."

"*Oui, monsieur.*" Bishou slid over to the driver's side. He had left the keys in the ignition. Quickly she turned the car around, and drove toward Saint-Denis.

There was a dearth of street signs, but she made an educated guess and saw a three-story house before her. She breathed a sigh of relief, however, when she spotted Louis's secretary standing before the building.

Claire spotted her boss's car at the same moment, and hurried to the curb. "Mademoiselle Bishou?!" she exclaimed.

"Please, I am to take you to the factory to send a cable," Bishou told her. "The tobacco has rust, and you are to request the antibiotic."

Claire simply dropped whatever she had been doing, and climbed into the passenger seat.

"Give me directions," said Bishou, "this is all too new to me."

"*Bien sûr,*" said Claire, pointing her down a couple of side streets and out to the road again. Once underway, Bishou explained what happened.

"It is good that Monsieur Dessant is with the workers," Claire said. "There will be no panic or anxiety if he is there. His hand is steady. Monsieur Campard, sometimes he lets them see how worried he is. Not Monsieur Dessant." This was probably more than the good secretary would admit within the walls of the factory.

"I know," said Bishou. "The crown has been jostled a bit, but he is still a king."

"Oui." Claire smiled. "I am not telling you anything new, am I? This is good. If we telephoned Paris today, on a Sunday, we might get anyone, and they might say anything. If we are in a queue of Monday-morning cables, we have more of a chance of being taken seriously by the university. I will also be on the telephone to them Monday morning, believe me."

"I believe you." Bishou drew up at the guards' cubicle. That car, those women—the guard waved her through. They were at the main doors in a heartbeat, where another security man let them inside.

The place was Sunday silent. It was queer to be in that still place, as it was to be walking purposefully down a corridor in her Sunday best with a secretary in capri pants, flats, and a sailor shirt.

Claire cranked up the electricity on a console-sized teletype machine against a wall, made sure its roll of paper was in position, and pulled out some papers from her desk. Carefully she assembled and wrote down her text. "I don't do this often enough to cable free-hand," she admitted, "so I like to have things ready." Next, she seated herself at the console, and began typing. There was clunky give and take, give and take, so the overseas communication device was functioning. At last, she started a long burst of typing, and nodded, satisfied, when she finished.

"We'll wait for the acknowledgement," she said. "It will probably take a few minutes, especially on a Sunday." Claire smiled at Bishou, who sat anxiously in the other chair. "Welcome to the tobacco-man's world, mademoiselle."

Bishou nodded. "Sick plants and machetes, balanced by his name on a box."

Claire laughed. "Oui. And those of us who do what we can, to keep the miracle going."

This time, Bishou laughed. "It does get in one's blood, doesn't it?"

"Certainly it does. This is the best job I could ever have." Her smile faded. "But I admit I was hired upon his return."

"That was probably good, that you were new then."

"Oui. I think so. So many people said, 'I remember when,' and I was free to say, 'But I was not here. I need the here-and-now.'" Tentatively, she added, "Perhaps you are like that, too."

Bishou nodded. "I think so. You and I, tobacco-women together." She gazed at a photo of Louis on the wall. "Was that for a promotional advertisement, that picture?"

"Oui. You have none?"

"No, not a photo of him. I don't think he has one of me, either."

"He has one, because I saw it."

Bishou stared. "Really?"

"Oui, he showed it when he first came back from America."

"The World Tobacco Conference at my university? I remember! The East Virginia University photographers took group photographs. I never got any, though, just the members of the conference." No, her only images of the quiet French widower were in her memory, but they had been enough to make her want to find him again. She did not need a photograph to see those brown eyes, that dark, wavy hair, that shy smile.

Claire smiled again, and was about to speak when the hammering of the terminal interrupted her. She read the notice. "Ah. Acknowledgement of receipt by the Sorbonne. We don't have a reply yet, but we know they received it. There is nothing more we can do today." She stood. Bishou followed suit. "And I promised I would take care of my nieces this afternoon."

"I'll take you back." Bishou nodded.

"Many thanks, Mademoiselle Bishou—" she laughed, "—not Mademoiselle for much longer, though!"

Bishou took Claire back to her street, and then found her way down the roads to the field where she had left the men. She knew for certain where she was only by a suit jacket, left hanging on a tree near the road. She pulled the car over, shut off the ignition, climbed out, and began to walk into the field.

The men were much further back now, no longer near the road. Louis, shirt sleeves rolled up, was chopping as determinedly and competently as the men around him. François saw Bishou approaching, and spoke to Louis. He straightened up, and they walked toward her.

Several men stopped working and gathered around them. "Mademoiselle Aucoeur has sent a request to the Sorbonne for the medicine," Bishou reported. "We know they have received the message, but, of course, no one will respond until tomorrow morning. She will telephone them in the morning as well."

"Good." Louis wiped his brow with his sleeve. "We'll keep doing as I said, François, just cut out the worst, and leave the mild rust in that back field to try the antibiotic on. I'd rather save it than destroy it, but above all, we must not let the rust spread."

"Oui. And we'll use different shovels for the different fields, too," said François. "I never thought about that, contagious like a cold." Apparently, Louis was even managing to teach some of his new findings to his crew.

"Do you need me here, or have you got men enough?"

"Non, monsieur, if we're not going to take out the back field, I've got enough men, but merci. You know, there are not many tobacco-men that can take it from the telephone to the machete."

"Both are business tools at Dessant," joked Louis, and all the men laughed.

Then one of the men said, "Best wishes to you both, Monsieur et Madame—tobacco-man and tobacco-man's wife." Other deep male voices muttered agreement.

Louis smiled down at Bishou as she replied, "Thank you for your good wishes, gentlemen." Then they returned to the car.

He picked up his suit coat from the tree. "I was afraid you would not be able to find us."

"I was glad your jacket was there."

"My apologies for testing you by fire." Louis saw her into the passenger seat, then seated himself in the driver's. He slid the machete back in the door pocket. "It would have been quite different if you could not drive this car."

"I know. But I could."

"François said to me, 'The lady cannot wait while you help us, monsieur.' I said, 'She understands tobacco.' And he replied, 'God bless you and may you both be happy in a tobacco-man's life.'" Louis kept his eyes on the road as he drove away, but his voice caught in his throat. "I think that blessing meant more to me than any I shall ever get from a church."

"And well it should," she agreed.

Louis pulled up at last in front of Pension Étoile, turned, and kissed her. "I needed that exercise. I think I will sleep well tonight, perhaps even this afternoon. We accomplished everything we intended, and then some, did we not?"

"Oui." Bishou kissed him again.

"Mm," he said, well pleased. "We still have the dress problem to consider, hm?"

"I suppose so."

"I like this church dress of yours. If all else fails, wear that. I wouldn't care if you wore a white djibbah with those nice high heels, truthfully. It is all *réunionnais*. Don't let it worry you. Sleep, *ma cherie*."

Louis escorted her to the door and kissed her yet again, like the lovers they were, before he said farewell. Inside the lobby, she sighed and felt the full force of her day's adventures.

Marie was on duty. She said, "You look tired, Mademoiselle Bishou."

"I am exhausted. What a day. And it is not yet two o'clock. I am going to sleep, Marie. Don't worry about noise. Nothing will wake me."

Chapter 3

Bishou slept through the night. The first noise she heard was the horn of the ferry *Mauritius Pride*, at nine o'clock the following morning. She rolled over and yawned.

Bishou had slept soundly. *Perhaps every day will not be like yesterday,* she thought, *but I know I can measure up to it. So does Louis.*

She staggered out of bed and down the hall to the bathroom, not worried about her looks or other travelers at nine o'clock in the morning. She brushed her teeth and hair, washed her face, and found her way back to her room.

Inside, she changed to her academic clothes because this would be a university day. She needed to go to the university library and research material for her Wednesday talk. Dressed but stocking-footed, she heard the tap-tap on the door and assumed it was Marie or Eliane. "*Entrez!*"

The tap-tap was repeated. Puzzled, Bishou opened the door.

A large drawing pad met her sight. The illustrated woman on it could have been Bishou. She wore a little white hat and veil much like Bishou's Sunday hat, and a white dress with a high collar, but otherwise much like the elegant blue dress Bishou had admired in the local dress shop the other day, before she left in anger over Nadine's scornful words. The dress had lace bunched up in back, probably ready to be released as a lightweight train. She wore the shoes Bishou had purchased.

Bishou looked up from the illustration to the face above the board. "'Great talent demolishes all barriers,'" she quoted.

Madame Nadine smiled. The hatchet was buried. "May I come in, Professor?"

"Please." Bishou motioned her inside.

"My apologies for my words to you Saturday. I am afraid we started off on the wrong footing."

"Ah, madame, let me apologize as well," Bishou replied. She could be noble, too. "I am trying to accomplish so much, in such a hurry. It is a very stressful time for me, and my temper grows too short."

Nadine sat down in the only chair, and glanced around her. Naturally, the open wardrobe door caught her attention. "Ah! What is that robe?"

"My doctoral gown." Bishou pulled it down for her to touch. "It was wrinkled in the package. Everything I brought with me was either in packages, or in my backpack. I came with nothing else."

Nadine stared. "And nothing else? To your wedding?"

"No, to my job. My work here was planned. My marriage was not."

"But you knew Monsieur Dessant before, I heard. You did not simply encounter him on a pleasure trip to Île de la Réunion."

"I was his translator at East Virginia University, when he came to a conference there. He fell ill, and I corresponded with the Campards to assist him. So, I came here, to see how he fared and to meet the Campards." Bishou sat on an edge of the bed and regarded her guest. "You have researched me, Mme. Nadine."

An elegant shrug. "I asked around. Mme. Ross told me much about you. Her assistant, *la noire*, knew of you, too. Apparently you are already a friend of the bus drivers."

"A word of advice," said Bishou. "*La noire's* name is Ceci. America is already suffering from race riots. Let your name be known for equality in your work."

"Don't lecture me," Mme. Nadine said sharply.

"I do not. I merely observe," Bishou replied evenly. "But if the race riots ever reach La Réunion—and anything is possible—it would be nice to own the one shop without broken windows."

"Mmph." Nadine made a non-committal, non-politick noise that became her. "And, of course, everyone saw you buy the shoes he wanted you to wear, and saw the sapphire he chose for you. Also the little diamond chevrons you are wearing."

"And will continue to wear." Bishou touched her necklace, which stayed with her even as she slept.

"And Monsieur Dessant?"

"I love him with all my heart."

The strength of her reply seemed to surprise Nadine. Bishou waited. At last, Nadine said thoughtfully, "*Bien*. Can you come to the shop this afternoon, around three? Bring your shoes. And we will fit the blue dress for your Wednesday night reception." *She certainly has done her homework*, Bishou thought. *That had to be a phone call to Claire or Bettina, or Louis himself, to dredge up that information.* "We can also take more accurate measurements for your wedding dress, so I can start the cutters on that. You prefer lace to voile? It is more expensive, you know."

"I know. What would you like for a down payment?"

Nadine named a figure that fitted Bishou's purse. Bishou counted out the cash. Nadine gave her a receipt. Purely coincidence, of course, that she happened to have her receipt book with her, as well as her sketch materials. "The balance will be due at the final fitting. That will be today for the blue dress, and tomorrow for the white one."

"*Oui, madame.*" Bishou stood. "*Et merci.*"

"*De rien.* I shall see you at three, then."

"*Oui, madame.*"

Mme. Nadine gathered up her materials, smiled over her shoulder, and left. Bishou felt a great weight lift from her shoulders. A few moments later, she too went downstairs.

The two genteel middle-aged pension hostesses were watching for Bishou. Eliane and Marie waved her in behind the counter, to their little breakfast table. "Well? Well? What did she say?"

"My blue dress will be ready for the reception Wednesday night, and the white one for Friday."

"Mon Dieu!" Eliane exclaimed. "She never takes two commissions at once from the same customer."

Marie concurred. "She must have been shaking in her boots, for fear the house of Dessant would snub her."

"Well, I am sure I don't know the answer. But I liked both designs, and she is a true artist." If the gossip lines worked in one direction, they probably worked in the other. Nadine would know by noontime that the Professor was saying nice things about her.

"And the church is all set?" Marie asked anxiously.

"Oui."

"I hope you don't mind, we spoke to the Père."

Bishou smiled, ate a bite of their wonderful croissants, and drank coffee. "Oh, you did? You and how many others, I wonder?"

"Oh, the Campards, I'm sure—they usually go to early Mass—and Mme. Nadine, she commented on your hat and wondered if you always wore hats like that—" Marie giggled. "I suppose we are a little responsible for the dress, eh?"

"More than a little responsible. I will wear it and think of you," Bishou promised. She set down her cup, excused herself, gathered up her portfolio bag, and left for the bus stop.

Soon she was at UFOI, the Université Français de l'Océan Indien. Bishou found the library. The darkness and smell of old leather was soothing and enticing. She found a study desk and began researching in earnest for her upcoming "Bible as Literature" lecture.

She became absorbed in her work. Other students came and went at her study table, usually just reading today's newspaper, or making notes of one kind or another. She wrote, timed her text, wrote more clearly, and wished she had a typewriter available. Ah, well. One thing that wouldn't fit in a backpack.

Bishou became aware of someone behind her only as he bent over and kissed her neck, just beneath her ear. She smiled up at Louis, stroked his hair, and touched her lips to enjoin silence. He nodded, and waited while she gathered everything back into her bag. They went out the front entrance to the library steps. Immediately he pulled out a cigarette. After his first puff, he handed it to her.

"Whew. Thank you," she said. "I am happy to see you. You are a welcome diversion."

"I am glad to serve my purpose. How is the researching?" Louis blew a puff of smoke into the sunny, clear air.

"Very good. I think I am ready."

"You are always ready." Another puff. "I wanted to let you know, Nadine has been looking for you."

"How do you know?"

"She called Bettina and pumped her while we were gone yesterday." Bettina and Madeleine, his housekeeper and cook, were also his secretaries, door guards, and surrogate mothers, at times.

"Ah, that explains much. She was at my door this morning."

Louis was surprised. "Bettina did not tell her where you were staying, Bishou. As a matter of fact, she spoke to me because she was afraid Nadine might harass you."

"Nadine found me, she came, and she behaved herself. She also got two commissions from me, which I understand is unheard of." She took another two puffs of his cigarette as they leaned against the stone railing of the library steps.

His dark eyes wistful, he asked, "The wedding dress?"

"Oui, she has designed it. I gave her a down payment. I go for a fitting tomorrow afternoon."

"What can you tell me about it?" he asked, in the same wistful tone.

She suppressed a smile. "Well...it's white."

Louis growled, grabbed her, brought her close, and kissed her. Bishou giggled. "This is not a good example for a professor to set."

"I am not a professor. They had better get used to it." He hugged her, and released her. A couple of students, sitting on a bench nearby, were grinning at them. "It is not...it is different, is it not?"

She answered the question he did not ask. "Yes, it is not like Carola's. I made sure."

"I am glad," Louis said softly. "I want this to be distinctly different. Have you seen the photograph? In Savridges' window?" Louis meant the photo shop on Rue Marché.

"I didn't really examine it. I saw it in the window."

"After ten years, it's still there. I hope...it would be nice if, someday, he trades it out for a photograph of the second Mme. Dessant. But mentioning it would only make things worse."

"Probably so. If there were only a couple photographs, you and me together, Louis, and maybe the boys with us, if they come, and the Campards...things that will always be happy memories of that day—that is all I would like. Not to faint from photo-fatigue."

"And a wedding-breakfast afterward, on our lawn? That would be nice. And it would be easy enough for Bettina and Madeleine to arrange."

"Yes, let's do that, if they don't mind."

"They won't mind. In fact, they asked me about our plans. They're looking forward to doing more entertaining than I do. They'll hire some help."

"Good. Oh," she said guiltily. "I may need to borrow some money from you, or Bat."

"*Borrow?*" he exclaimed.

"The wedding dress is going to cost more than I thought. And I haven't done my hair yet, or even looked at flowers."

"You little idiot," Louis said indignantly, "do you think you are paying for all this?"

"I have a job—"

"You are my wife. Whose pride shall be sacrificed, yours or mine?" Louis demanded.

Faced with that, she replied meekly, "Mine."

Louis made a very French, very husbandly, noise, and gathered her into his arms. "I should think so. My pride already has a dent in it, from having a wife who works. I console myself with the fact that she is a professor, *une docteur*, and she is special. But really, Bishou, I have limits."

"Good." She smiled, and touched his face. "Good." She kissed him. Bishou did not want to let Louis pay for everything, as Carola had—before she'd absconded with his bank accounts as well. Bishou had no intention of setting a precedent. She did not want to take advantage of him, but his male vanity had taken a terrible hit when Carola robbed him blind.

After a second kiss, Louis mused, "You know—if you do borrow money from me...I can take it in trade, hein?"

Bishou laughed. "Oui, it's in the contract."

"You will come to dinner tonight, *chez moi?*"

She teased, "Do we need a chaperone?"

Louis grinned. "Only if you have an old Parisian aunt. In Réunion, non. But I do not promise to keep my hands to myself, as they say in Virginia."

"It sounds worse in French. All right, I have a dress appointment at Nadine's at three, and then I will come to your place."

"Shall I pick you up at Nadine's?"

"Don't you have a job?"

"Oui," he admitted sheepishly, "I do. But the boss is amenable to me."

"Go to work. I'll finish my appointment, and take the bus out to Rue Dessant."

"All right. Another kiss," he demanded. He kissed her, and left.

Bishou smiled and shook her head. Louis had come out here

just to warn her about Nadine. He was curious about this new job, and the university. He was curious about the dress, which he shouldn't see until the wedding. He was acting so damn normal, and enjoying his chance to just wallow in it.

The young couple was still watching her. She grinned at them, too, and got return grins. This university felt comfortable. She would be all right here.

Bishou made her way to the front gate, and waited for the bus. "Bonjour, Papa Armand!" she greeted the driver, climbing on and paying him. "How many children do you have working the bus routes?"

"Five now," chuckled the Creole, also accepting a cigarette. "Friday is the day, eh, mam'selle? And you are marrying a rich man. You will not need this job, then, after all?"

"I'm going to do it anyway," Bishou answered, seating herself comfortably in a forward seat. "Good to have the practice, you know—and I will have 'pocket money,' a little money of my own that my husband won't need to provide for me. Fair is fair."

"You know about Monsieur Dessant's wife, how she cheated him?" Armand asked.

"Yes."

"Man's made some mistakes," Armand said. She recognized a euphemism for prison time.

"Lots of good men do," Bishou replied.

"Ain't scaring you," said Armand.

Bishou made another inspired guess. "*You* don't."

Armand glanced at her, looking a little surprised. Then he chuckled. A while later, he chuckled again, a deep throaty chuckle. Sure enough, Louis Dessant wasn't the only jailbird on the island who was now working hard to make things right. Louis hadn't been mistaken when he said the Père issued dispensations in packets. "Where you going today, Mam'selle Bishou?"

"Rue Marché. Nadine's."

"Wedding dress!"

"And another fancy dress, too."

"You getting all your clothes from her?"

"Non. There's another shop I like better. When you look at me, do you see a dainty little Frenchwoman?"

Armand chuckled again. "Non, mam'selle, God made you good."

"*Merci*. But you see I must wear a little bit of this, a little bit of that."

"Oui, I see. But you're *étrangère* to the island. You let me know what you need, Mam'selle, and I'll see if I can find you the right help."

"I'll remember that, Armand, I promise."

Bishou walked down Rue Marché from the bus stop, carrying her tote bag and her purse. In the tote bag was her work portfolio, but also her new shoes.

Nadine and the other saleswoman were both waiting for her, this time. Bishou had an uncomfortable flashback of the other married couple, the other day, as they were fawned over while Bishou was ignored.

As Bishou had said, the blue dress fit fairly well. She donned the elegant shoes. Nadine fiddled with a side tuck, and her assistant pinned the hem. "It must be fairly easy for me to get in and out of, alone," said Bishou, "because I will very likely be changing my clothes in a ladies' room off the college entrance."

Nadine sighed. "You may need help with the hooks."

"I will get help."

"And those are the shoes you will be wearing, and that is the jewelry."

"Oui."

"All right, they will go together well enough with the blue dress."

"And with the white?"

"That too. One problem at a time."

"It is all one problem," said Bishou. "I am la deuxième Madame Dessant." She emphasized "second," and met Nadine's gaze steadily.

"I understand," said Nadine, but her assistant dropped her pincushion in consternation and grabbed it hastily before it rolled under the stool. "Neither you nor Monsieur are made of stone, are you?"

"'If you prick us, do we not bleed?'" Bishou quoted, obligingly translating Shakespeare into French.

"Not on *my* fabric," said Nadine intently—then realized what she had said. They both burst into laughter.

*

Bishou was walking up Rue Dessant when she realized that Louis was walking down to meet her. He took the larger parcels out of her hands. "How could you have seen me?"

"I was upstairs." He rustled a package he carried. "What is this?"

"The dress for Wednesday night."

"And this?"

"Lingerie."

"Oh ho. Sexy and revealing, I hope."

"Well—yes, or it would show badly under the dress."

"I am encouraged. You do not display your charms."

"You must show me what you want from me," she said simply.

He smiled and said nothing. In the house, Bettina welcomed her and set her things on the coat rack with her packages, then returned to the kitchen.

Suddenly, Louis grabbed her, pressed her against the hallway wall, and kissed her savagely. She felt his hands stroking her body. She kept her arms around his neck and returned his kisses, but he was neither calmed nor soothed. His hands pushed and gripped. He kissed her throat, forcing her head back as he kissed and bit. He was out of control. She struggled ineffectively, gasping.

Then he took a deep shuddering breath, and became calm. His grip was still strong, but steady. In her ear, he murmured, "Oh, *mon amour*, I am going mad with the wait."

"Louis," she urged softly, "come. *Reste ici.* We are both going mad."

Slowly, he released her. She took his hand, led him to his own couch, and sat down with him.

Louis drew her into his arms. He brushed her hair back from her face. He drew her legs over onto his lap, and kissed her again—gently, this time. "I hadn't meant to—rough you up so much."

"You startled me more than anything."

"I did not frighten you?"

"Non," she lied. "My only thought was, this is not our wedding night."

Louis smiled and touched her lips with his fingers, recognizing the lie. "I promise not to lose control again."

"Before the wedding," she amended.

He acquiesced. "Before the wedding. Afterward, I make no guarantees."

"I would not ask for more, *mon mari*."

"I want to hear you call me '*mon mari*,' and mean it, in our bed. I want to hear you say it after the loving." Louis touched her face, and looked in her eyes. "I wanted to give you a tour of the rest of the house tonight, and ask you which room you wanted for our bedroom. Maybe not the same one I have always used, I thought."

"That might be a good idea. I don't know." Bishou gentled her voice to match his tone. His hand was under her skirt, stroking her thigh.

"But now I am afraid that the moment you look at a bedroom you like and say, '*Ah, oui*,' I won't be able to restrain myself."

"'*Ah, oui*'? Is that your sex cue?"

"For lovemaking? Ah, oui," Louis said, with a twinkle in his eye.

Bishou thought of the number of times she had kissed him, and heard him say those very words. He had been telling her yes all along, and she hadn't realized it. In an odd way, she felt as if she had wronged him.

Bishou shifted their positions on the couch until he lay with his head in her lap. She rested her arms around him and made sure he was comfortable. He stroked her blouse at the breast. The smile never left his lips. He still wore his tie, a white four-in-hand. She loosened the knot and removed it, then unbuttoned his shirt enough to slip her hand inside. She felt warm skin and the movement of his chest as he breathed. *This is my man*, she thought, *mon mari*.

"*Qu'est-ce que tu pensais?*"

"I like touching you."

His smile grew. "I am glad. It feels good, too. And, tomorrow, you buy the wedding dress."

"Oui. Tomorrow."

"Are you excited?"

Her smile matched his. "Yes, very. More about the man than the dress."

"Oh, what of the man?" he teased.

"A luscious, sexy tobacco-man."

Louis laughed. "Now you make fun of me."

Bettina appeared long enough to say that dinner was served. They made their way to the dining room. While they ate, Bishou worried about where her brothers would stay. Louis said pfah, let them stay here, plenty of room on the top floor. She wondered if Denise and Etien would be their witnesses; Louis said he would ask tomorrow, but he assumed so. She told Louis who she planned to ask about her hair; he told her where to buy a bouquet. They probably conducted more bridal business at that supper table than either had accomplished the rest of the week.

They climbed the stairs. Louis showed her the upstairs bathroom, with its spacious tub—"room for two," he murmured in her ear, and his bedroom on that floor.

"Whew," she said, staring at the white French Provincial furniture, "like something out of a mail-order catalog, isn't it?"

"I think my grandparents brought the suite with them from France." He opened the window to the balcony. "Not much of a view, either. What you see from here is the driveway."

"Where were you looking for me, today?"

"Upstairs." He led the way to the top floor. Here were two bedrooms—one a modest double-bedded guest room, and one containing a generous bed with a colorful print cover in a room with African touches. He opened the window on this room, and stepped onto the balcony with her. "You see, a much better view."

Bishou turned back to look inside. "I like this room, Louis. It's comfortable."

He smiled and admitted, "It was my childhood room, although the furniture has changed and my childhood things are long gone. Bettina and Madeleine refurnished it—while I was away."

"Really?" She looked up into his face in wonder. "They kept the house up?"

"For me. Yes, they did. And reported to Etien and Denise, and went on half-wages until I returned."

"What loyalty!"

"When I returned—it was the only thing that made me weep. Them, too, I admit." He nuzzled and kissed her, and added, "Do you know, I went downstairs to the kitchen yesterday—just to refill my coffee cup—and Bettina was sitting at the kitchen table, weeping. I was alarmed. I gave her my handkerchief and asked her why she cried. She said, 'Oh, Monsieur, I heard you singing.' I asked, 'Was I that bad?' and she answered, 'No, it's that you never sang before Mademoiselle Bishou. Your heart is mending.'"

"I'm glad to hear it," Bishou said softly.

Louis pulled her over to the bed, and sat on one edge with her, his arm around her waist. "Very good," he said, in the same soft tone. "We will have this room, and this bed. The moon will shine in our balcony window, and in the morning, we will see the roads and the fields all the way to Saint-Denis. *D'accord?*"

"*D'accord.*"

Then Louis drove her and her packages back to the pension. "Not this much longer, ma Bishou," he said, as he kissed her at the door. "Then we just go upstairs."

"Soon," she promised. "*Bonne nuit.*"

One last kiss. "*Bonne nuit.*"

Bishou went inside. She heard the car drive off. It seemed harder tonight to leave him, somehow.

"*Bonjour*, Mademoiselle Bishou," said Joseph cheerfully. "I was waiting until you came in to bar the door."

"I am glad you knew I would be back," said Bishou. "It was very difficult to leave him tonight."

Joseph smiled at her. "He is a lucky man, mademoiselle."

"You are very kind."

"You sound sad. No homework tonight, mademoiselle," Joseph advised. "Sleep instead."

"You may be right, Joseph. *Bonne nuit.*"

"*Bonne nuit*, mademoiselle."

She climbed the stairs to her room, washed up, changed her clothes, and called it a night.

Chapter 4

Tuesday. She heard the deep horn of the ferry. For a few minutes, she lay in bed, feeling the longing. It would be nice to be able to touch him, to say, "Wake up, let's start our day." And she hadn't heard from Bat, either. *Well, do things that are within your control, Bishou,* she told herself. *Order your flowers, get your wedding dress finished, finish your lecture notes, see about your hair. And what else to while away your time?*

"Mademoiselle Eliane, may I use your telephone?"

She dialed a number from her notebook, and heard, "Campard residence."

"May I speak to Mme. Campard? This is Bishou Howard."

"Oui, *Professeur*, un moment." The receiver jiggled; a voice murmured in the background. Then a new voice came on the line.

"*Allo*, Bishou! Denise Campard *ici*."

"Denise, may I invite myself to lunch with you? I feel like I haven't seen you in weeks."

"Oh, I'd love it! But here's what we will do instead. This is my day to volunteer at the library. Then we'll meet for lunch at Chez Ma Tante, the little café next to it, and I'll treat you. Is that all right?"

"That's a wonderful idea," said Bishou.

"Are you spending too much time with your own thoughts?"

"That's it, exactly."

"Well, come to the library, then, and help me mend books. We can always use an extra hand. I volunteer at the main library on Mango Street."

"That's the best idea I've heard in days."

Denise laughed. "The library is open in the afternoon and

evening, and we volunteers work in it mornings. Come to the front door and ring the bell. We'll keep an eye out for you. I'll be there in about half an hour."

"All right, I'll see you then." After she hung up the phone, she asked Eliane, "Where's Mango Street?"

"Six or seven blocks straight uphill. Are you going to the public library? Go up from here, then make a left at the Mango Street sign. You'll see a little café nearby, too, Chez Ma Tante." That jibed with what Denise had said. "The library is a nice little place—not like the university library, of course—but a comfortable place to read a magazine or a mystery book. I go there sometimes, myself."

Her directions were good, and Bishou was satisfied with the uphill exercise. She had spent too much time sitting around. The public library was a nondescript building, sand and stucco and cement, but the doors were clearly marked and she found the doorbell easily enough. She saw the shadowy outline of a slim woman with glasses, walking swiftly to the door, unquestionably Denise's silhouette. The door opened before she rang, and Denise Campard ushered her inside.

Denise took Bishou to a back room, where something like a quilting bee was going on—only it was a book-mending bee, with six women industriously gluing and taping.

"Girls, this is my friend Bishou," said Denise. The ladies responded with a chorus of hellos.

"New to town, Bishou?" asked one.

"Yes," Bishou replied. Denise merely smiled, pushed up her spectacles, and showed Bishou some bookmending basics.

Bishou worked with tape, glue, spacing sticks, and other tools, and listened to the conversation. One woman had just had a baby. Another had a grandchild who had just begun to walk. Another woman was training a new dog. The conversations were mellow and unimportant, interspersed with questions about how to best save the cover of this book or a signature in that one. Bishou felt herself relax. She met Denise's gaze, and saw her smile.

In a low voice, Denise asked, "How have things gone?"

"Busy but productive," Bishou answered. "I'm just tired, that's all."

"I can imagine. Etien told me about meeting you at the University. He would have felt silly if you hadn't taken it so well."

"You married a wonderful man," said Bishou.

"And you are going to," Denise replied, in an undertone, patting her hand.

One of the ladies saw the gesture, and laughed. "You are one of Denise's lost souls, aren't you, Bishou? Any time anyone has a problem, Denise says, come in here and mend books, it will make you feel better."

Bishou gave her a big smile. "That's it, exactly. I feel like I owe Denise a lot, so what's a little glue for repayment?"

The girls laughed. Another woman marched into the back room and said, "Good morning, ladies!"

"Good morning, Madame Cantrell."

Her gaze fell on Bishou, and she said loudly, "Ah! We have a new volunteer this morning! Welcome! And you are?"

"Madame, allow me to introduce my friend, Bishou."

"Bishou, eh? Do you have a last name, Bishou?"

"*Oui, madame,*" said Bishou, and concentrated on the book she was mending, somehow omitting to mention it.

Denise merely giggled. "Come on, Bishou, you're teasing Madame. I know you better than that."

Bishou looked up at the matron, and smiled slightly. She certainly wouldn't embarrass Denise Campard, or call her a liar. "I do, madame. It's Howard."

"Howard, eh?" the woman said, equally loudly. "Where have I—ah! I know. The university sent out an announcement about a lecture open to the public that is being given by a Docteur Howard. Any relation to you?"

"Yes, I'm related," Bishou replied. She saw Denise clamp her lips tightly to keep from laughing.

"So we'll see you at the lecture?"

"Definitely," Bishou replied.

"'The Bible as Literature.' Sounds a little agnostic, but who knows. My husband and I will certainly be there. We do everything we can to support art and culture in Saint-Denis. Does your husband, as well?"

"My husband can take it or leave it," Bishou replied. "Sometimes I must coax him a little."

In a stage whisper, with a great wink, Mme. Cantrell boomed, "Mine too. See you at the lecture."

Denise bent down under the table, ostensibly to pick up something from her purse, until the great woman proceeded out the door. Then Bishou turned to Denise and whispered, "Who the hell was that?"

"Chairwoman of the Library Society," said Denise, collapsing in silent laughter. "Stopping by to see how we are doing. Come on, I've got to get you out of here while I can still walk."

"I'm really sorry," Bishou said, as they seated themselves at an outside café table. "I didn't mean to make a scene among your friends."

"You didn't," said Denise gleefully. "They'll have caught on by next week. Bishou, I love you dearly."

"Good. It makes it easier for me to ask you to be my bridesmaid."

"Gladly." Denise didn't seem surprised. "I wondered if you were hesitating just because I was present the first time."

"You mean Carola, pretending to be Celie Bourjois?"

"Oui, Carola the false bride. Do you have a particular dress in mind for me?"

"Non. Have you got a blue dress?"

"Yes. Any particular shade of blue?"

"No, not really. Just blue. And be there. It's all I ask."

"I'm glad you're not picky. And when is your family coming? Will you need a guest room for them?"

"I think not. Louis says they'll stay at the house, with us. But my younger brothers must be about the same age as your boys. I hope they'll spend time together."

"That will be good. We'll invite them over. This is so exciting, Bishou. Excuse me for saying it—a *real* Madame Dessant." She reached out and clasped Bishou's hand. "How is Louis taking all this?"

"It's been a little difficult for him, but he's happy."

"Difficult how?"

Bishou told her about the trip to the church, and a little about their talks in the dark and on the coast road. "He is trying very hard not to let old ghosts spoil anything for him, but every once in a while, we unwittingly conjure one up."

"I know," said Denise. "Louis never told us everything Carola did to him, or what happened in the prisons, no more than he tells you. He keeps many things in his heart. We've always had him over for Friday night dinner—some weeks are good, some are not. But, you know, the boys love him, and so do we."

"Does it bother you—" Bishou struggled for the words and found none, "—if the boys don't inherit from him?" Shy Etien Campard was Louis' oldest friend, school chum, and (as much as he hated managing the company) business partner. He had stood by Louis through all his tough times, as staunchly as any brother. Louis, an only child, a lonely widower, was immensely grateful for Etien's friendship.

"Pardon?" Denise stared at her.

"Does it—" Bishou repeated, and then stopped in surprise. "Am I telling you something you don't know, Denise? I don't mean to be a cow about this." *Quelle vache*, she thought, *Denise doesn't know.*

"*Inherit* from him?" Denise repeated in shock.

"Oui. His will states that if he dies without issue, his share of Dessant Cigarettes goes to Jean-Luc and Pierrot Campard, equally."

"Sacré Nom," mild-mannered Denise swore wholeheartedly, "I certainly hope you plan to have children. We have already spent our ten years in hell."

"Louis said that was how Etien felt about it, but I wanted to make sure."

"He got that right," Denise affirmed. "Oh mon Dieu, Bishou, you don't know what it was like. Running the business, and fighting blight, Louis on the run with Carola, her suicide, and his arrest. And then prison. There seemed to be no hope. I thought Etien's heart would break. And I was so helpless. *We* were so helpless."

"I understand," said Bishou.

"I'm so glad you do. There are plenty of other women who would say, 'It is just business. My husband will handle it.' That simply isn't true. When I heard that Louis sent you to fetch Claire, to help him out, I wanted to shout for joy. It is not only that you helped him. It is that he reached out for your help."

"He never thought twice about it. It was work, his business," said Bishou.

"*Hein?* Do you think he would have sent *me* running off to the factory to send a cable? Or even Carola? And expect the task to be accomplished with no problems?" Again, she gripped Bishou's hand. "It's only you, Bishou, who could do that. You don't let him down. He trusts you. And that's a lot to say, for someone who's been through everything he has."

"Denise," Bishou protested, but her heart wasn't in it, "he's perfectly capable."

"You know what I mean. He's coming back from whatever terrible place he was."

"I think you're right," said Bishou.

*

Bishou eyed herself uncertainly in the mirror, in the privacy of her own room. This underwear was certainly sexy, lacy, and revealing. No one else would know what was underneath her academic skirt and blouse but her. Still, it was not what she usually wore. She reminded herself that the blue dress would be required after the lecture, and her ordinary bra and panties might be too obvious, and might show through the fabric. And two sets of underwear, as well as the dress and two sets of shoes, was just too much to lug around. She was glad Louis was going to bring some things over for her and meet her in the parking area.

She caught the bus to the university stop, and hopped off at her destination. Inside the gates, she checked the campus bulletin board. There it was: "'The Bible as Literature,' Lecture by Professorial Candidate Docteur Bishou Howard. Wednesday, 1900 heures, Morison Lecture Hall 59." Hm. Any sign that she was female? Nope. Ah, well. That would change quick enough. This was, in its way, a job interview, and she was up for it.

She had checked, UFOI did not require academic garb while teaching. That was probably because it started out with an emphasis on science. If anything, scientists wore lab coats, not their academic robes, while lecturing. She was good in a white blouse with a black skirt and sensible pumps.

And, of course, academic attitude.

Bishou lifted her head and stepped confidently into the Morison Lecture Building. How they numbered the rooms was a mystery, because here was Room 59, almost inside the front entryway. Students were milling around, whether for her lecture or other classes, she could not tell. But she was being observed.

She reached Room 59 and saw that it was very similar to the lecture hall she had used at East Virginia University. Standing there was Dr. Rubin, as if she had had any doubt. With him were a circle of students, and a couple of men who looked too old to be students—probably other professors. Dr. Rubin stepped forward. "Ah, Docteur Howard. Welcome."

"*Bonjour*, Dr. Rubin."

"Allow me to introduce our Humanities Department faculty. Dr. Guillaume Robert. Dr. Pierre Castelle. Dr. Theodore du Verger. Dr. Claude-Marie Dukette. Dr. Albert Weis." They were all in their forties or fifties except Pierre Castelle, who looked like he might have just got out of school. They all greeted her, and shook her hand.

"I understand that it is a combined department, consisting of literature and philosophy," Bishou said to Dr. Rubin.

"I presume you had already gathered that, from the nature of your lecture," Dr. Rubin answered.

"Actually, no. My lecture is strictly literary, because that was my intention," she replied. Pierre Castelle flashed a quick grin. From his looks, she guessed that he was the department firebrand. He was the right age, also, to have been in the Paris student riots.

Students began drifting in, male and female. Some looked at Bishou in surprise. A couple left, and she could hear their voices outside the room. Dr. Rubin sent Pierre after a glass of water for her, another indication that he was low man on the totem pole. "So," said Pierre, as he handed her the glass and set a pitcher on the lectern, "are you going to tell us about the God-given properties of the Bible?"

"Wait and see," she replied good-humoredly.

Dr. duVerger said, "I'm trying to place your accent, and I cannot. Where are you from, if you don't mind telling?"

"I don't mind. I'm from Boston, Massachusetts, but my parents are originally from Quebec. I have tried to keep regionalisms out of my speech, but sometimes they appear. I'll know because you'll laugh."

"Dr. Rubin showed us your credentials," said Dr. Dukette.

"You are fresh out of East Virginia University. Are you ready to pick up a full academic load?"

"No," she replied. "I may only be adjunct for a while, so you can give me the courses you hate teaching."

Now they laughed.

Male and female students entered the hall. There were now a good thirty people there. They could hear the university clock chime seven. "Ready?" Dr. Rubin eyed her.

"Ready."

"I'll introduce you. Hm, that fellow in the tie-dye shirt is from the school paper. They fetched him. You'll be news, probably not for the first time."

"Probably not," she agreed. If they thought she was going to hyperventilate over an article about a woman professor, just wait until the *Journal de l'Île* broke the story of her marriage to Louis Dessant. This would be a drop in the bucket.

"Good evening, ladies and gentlemen. Welcome to the expository lecture of Dr. Bishou Howard, candidate for Professor of Comparative Literature. Dr. Howard's lecture this evening is titled 'The Bible as Literature.' Dr. Howard received her Master's degree in Comparative Literature from Bowling Green University and her doctoral degree in Comparative Literature from East Virginia University, both in the United States of America. She received her doctorate earlier this year. Her teaching and lecturing experience includes several American and Canadian universities. She has moved recently to Saint-Denis and hopes to establish herself in our Humanities Department. I hope you will join me in welcoming Dr. Howard to UFOI."

Bishou ignored the slight applause. College professors didn't expect applause. "Thank you, Dr. Rubin, it is an honor to be here. Now, I am going to make some assumptions regarding my audience, and the first is that you have at least a nodding acquaintance with some form of Christianity."

They laughed, but it was not an idle question. There were at least a couple of Oriental faces in this crowd, as well as Creole and Indian. She concentrated on her subject.

Bishou talked about the Bible as a book. Tabling the question of whether or not the content was God-given, she focused on the editorial skills that went into various versions, and the talent and intentions of those editors. Her audience, familiar with the Douay and other French versions, actually took notes as she spoke of other versions found throughout the world. The Jerusalem Bible, for instance, followed a timeline, and aligned itself with the construction, existence, and destruction of the Temple, as clearly as a literary diagram. She mentioned versions that served as "crib notes" for readers confused by the more flowery language of other versions, and how they often went back to those versions once they understood the plot or characters.

Also, according to her custom, Bishou did not hide behind a podium. She walked back and forth. Occasionally, she pointed into the audience, challenging someone to name the seven deadly sins or the Synoptic Gospels. She saw the library maven, Mme. Cantrell, and pointed to her, saying her name and challenging her to name the Seven Sacraments—which she did, laughing. Bishou shot out other questions, expecting answers, sometimes getting them, sometimes not, and then giving the answers herself.

As she spoke, she realized that she saw priests among the students—probably the college chaplain and his friends. Yes, surely the Creole man was Père Reynaud. He was smiling, too.

She talked about the insistence of the writers on Jesus' persistent simple faith in God his father, and compared the Beatitudes to "Arjuna's pep talk about Krishna" in the *Mahabharata*. Some Hindus and Sikhs in the audience brightened visibly. Again, people grabbed pencils and notebooks.

Bishou realized her hour was almost up. She encouraged serious students of inspirational literature to sit down and read, with equal time spent in thought or in the reading of commentaries. She opened the floor for questions.

Pierre's hand. "Dr. Howard, you spoke of passion. Is that not what your dissertation covered?"

"Passion in literature, yes. My dissertation was mainly a summary and compilation of the role that passion plays in major works of literature."

"Not in real life?"

"Real life is very difficult to footnote in a dissertation," she replied, amid more laughter.

A student's hand, male. "As a woman in the academic field, do you feel you are handicapped by your sex when it comes to such topics as passion and monasticism?"

"No, because I am dealing with fellow academics, not writing a populist book."

"Would it be a handicap writing a populist book?"

"I don't know, I haven't tried."

Another student asked if she had read the *Mahabharata* in the original. She replied no, and mentioned the translation she read. She was asked if she read Hebrew. Not enough to hold a conversation, she replied. Had she memorized the Koran? No. She read Anglicized versions, and knew the most famous quotes, but not the Koran in its entirety. There were more questions along these lines, really to see if she was a professor, she thought.

Then she said, "I think that about wraps up the lecture and the questions. If anyone has any other questions, please write them down and pass them on to the Humanities department here, and I will do my best to answer them. Thank you for being an excellent audience. I appreciate your sympathy and attention."

Another round of applause, much louder this time. She saw Louis in the back row, applauding too. The students left.

The professors remained. Dr. Rubin said, "Thank you very

much, Dr. Howard. I will be in touch with you or your friends tomorrow."

"The Campards will take a message for me if I am not there," Bishou replied. She shook his hand. "Thank you for giving me the opportunity to speak."

"Thank you for speaking," he said, equally politely. His glance rested on the man who had moved to the front of the hall to join them, a man in dress clothes. "Ah! Dr. Howard's guest, I presume."

"*Oui, Monsieur le Doyen,*" Louis replied with a smile.

"Then we shall see you at the Rare Books reception in a little while," said Dr. Rubin. "Monsieur—?"

"Dessant," said Louis.

"Ah. As in the cigarette?"

Louis smiled at the time-worn question. "*Oui,* as in the cigarette."

"A pleasure to meet you, Monsieur Dessant," said Dr. Rubin, as if it were the most natural thing in the world. "*À toute à l'heure.*"

"*À toute à l'heure,*" Louis replied, as he and Bishou left.

In the corridor, Louis said, "They know the cigarette, that is all, isn't it?"

"You aren't a major factor in their world," Bishou replied.

"And here you are, straddling both. Your dress-bag is in my car."

They walked out, together, to the university car park. Louis opened the trunk of the white Mercedes and pulled out Bishou's dress-bag. They returned to the lecture building, where Bishou made her way to the ladies' room. There, in the empty bathroom, she changed to the blue dress, put on her shoes, and applied evening makeup.

Bishou stepped out of the bathroom and saw Louis's eyes widen. She hadn't realized how much the elegant dress transformed her. "Could you hook this for me?"

"With pleasure." His hands were sure as he fastened the dress hooks. She felt his fingers touch the bare skin of her back before he finished his task. He slid his arms around her waist, drawing her back against him, and murmured in her ear, "You are quite beautiful."

"Only in your eyes," she said softly. She closed her eyes as he kissed her neck.

Chapter 5

They walked to the parking area. Bishou placed her clothing bag in the trunk of the open white car. She looked up in time to see Louis eyeing another car in the same lot. The car had government seals. "We might see people I know," Louis said, his voice sounding restrained.

"Such as?"

"My parole officer."

"Oh, really." What could she say to that?

"Mm, oui. I will probably introduce you to him, you know. Be warned."

"*Bien*, we are ready," Bishou replied. She took his arm as they re-entered university grounds and made their way to the library.

The library doors were open. Well-dressed students were standing by, ushering or directing nicely dressed visitors to the Clemenceau Rare Books Room. Bishou clasped Louis's elbow as if this were the most normal thing in the world, and they walked toward the Rare Books Room.

It was a large room crowded with people, certainly more than a Rare Books librarian would see on an ordinary working day. They could see a refreshments table, with stewards pouring wine, as they entered the door of the room. There were two or three groups of people, talking. Glass cases on tables displayed some of the library's existing treasures. Thirty or forty people milled around in this room, elegantly dressed, a striking contrast to the usual student garb one expected to see.

Bishou glanced at her companion, and thought: *He's perfect. Here's where he would be under normal conditions, at an elite reception.* Louis gazed at the people in the room, looking somehow inscrutable and urbane, the perfect escort.

Louis murmured, "Shall we get some wine?"

"Yes, let's."

They walked together to the refreshment table, where a steward poured wine. Louis snagged a stem of red wine for himself, and gave her the white.

On the other side of the room, Bishou noticed the Library Society chairwoman, Mme. Cantrell, making eye contact with her. "I think we need to speak to one of Denise's friends."

"Certainly, if you say so." Louis accompanied her to the little crowd around the assertive chairwoman.

"Bishou," said Mme. Cantrell, when they were close enough, "no wonder Mme. Campard was laughing at me when I asked if you were related to tonight's speaker. It was nice of you not to be rude to me."

"I didn't want to tease you, in a room full of people," said Bishou.

"Not much, you mean," Mme. Cantrell replied good-humoredly. "Well, I enjoyed your talk very much, and it gave me a good idea how lively those American classrooms must be."

"There are good days and bad days, like teaching anywhere," Bishou replied.

"No doubt there must be," said the gentleman next to Madame, who Bishou gathered to be Monsieur Cantrell. "It was a pleasure to hear you speak tonight, Docteur."

"Oh, that's right," said Mme. Cantrell, "you must be a Docteur, aren't you—or a Professeur?"

"Either, or both," replied Bishou.

"And your good husband!" Mme. Cantrell held out her hand to Louis. "I'm called Madame Cantrell—I'm the volunteer coordinator at the public library, in case Bishou didn't tell you."

"Not yet her husband," Louis contradicted with a smile. "We are to be married later this week. A pleasure to meet you, madame."

"Oh, my goodness!" Madame reproached Bishou, "all our idle talk, and you didn't put in a word that you were planning to be married this week! When?"

"Friday."

"Our good wishes," said her husband jovially, "and congratulations, mademoiselle, monsieur."

"Merci," Louis replied comfortably, patting Bishou's hand on his arm and looking at her fondly. "I am most fortunate."

At that moment, a voice called across the room, "Louis!" They turned to see a hand reaching up from one of the greater groups of people.

"Pardon, I am being summoned," said Louis, turning away from the group and walking in the direction of the others. *Louis's parole officer?* Bishou wondered.

"That looked like—surely that wasn't the Prefect himself who summoned him?" Mme. Cantrell asked with a frown. It certainly did look like Louis was speaking with the Prefect, the island's equivalent of a governor. Her frown faded as she looked once again at Bishou. "Your young man is quite handsome, Bishou."

"Thank you for noticing," Bishou agreed, "I think so, too."

"Are you excited about marriage?"

"Definitely."

"This is a first marriage for both of you?"

Good thing Denise wasn't here, Bishou thought, *she would be offended by now.* "My first, his second. My fiancé is a widower."

"How sad for him, how happy for you both."

Bishou had kept Louis in the corner of her eye, and now saw him raise his hand to motion to her. She excused herself to Mme. Cantrell's group, turned, and walked to him. For some reason, the gazes of the group she was approaching made her very conscious of her looks—her high-heeled shoes, her jewels, her body, her walk, the blue dress.

Louis reached out to take her hand, and said, "*Monsieur le*

Prefect, allow me to introduce my fiancée, Bishou Howard. Ma Bishou, this is the Prefect of Réunion Island, Monsieur Jean-Pierre Masson." She had not imagined it. The island governor was Louis's parole officer!

Bishou's eyes lit up with her smile. She held out her hand. "*Monsieur le Prefect*, it is a great honor to meet you. Thank you so much for all you have done for Louis."

The Prefect had the perfect little French goatee. Now, at closer quarters, she could also see his French governmental ribbons and badges of office. There was a twinkle in his eye. A slim woman beside him could only be his wife, and proved so upon introduction. She clung to Bishou's hand, and released it gently.

"Why, Louis, she's lovely!" said Madame with a smile, then to Bishou, "You are American?"

"Oui, Madame, from Boston, Massachusetts."

"Boston!" said the Prefect, "I have been there once. Shortly after the museum was robbed. Such a tragedy. Have they found the villains yet?"

"No, Monsieur, not yet, but they are still looking." That had been ten years ago.

"What do you think of our island?" his wife asked.

"I like it very much. I think I will be happy here," Bishou replied. "It is very like Virginia, where I studied."

"That's right," said the Prefect sheepishly, "you gave a lecture tonight, which—ahem—I skipped."

Bishou laughed. "I imagine the opportunity to skip a meeting is a great luxury for you, *Monsieur le Prefect*, so you must enjoy this little vacation."

"You are a good sport, Mademoiselle," the Prefect grinned, "or should I say Docteur? Or Professeur?" He seemed like an alert and capable politician.

"All are correct—for a few more days," Bishou replied. "Then it will no longer be Mademoiselle."

"So will you be Docteur Dessant, then?" his wife asked.

"There is paperwork to change, for my diploma and my contract, so it may be a while before I can use that name in my work," Bishou replied, "but that is the name I intend."

"The contracts for the university system run through government channels," said the Prefect. "Let me know if you need any help."

"Ah, Monsieur," Louis demurred, "as long as the wheels of government are turning, we will not disturb you with our petty problems. I am grateful for the assistance you have already given me. I wouldn't wish to pester you." He patted Bishou's hand.

Other men and women had been standing nearby. Bishou had not focused on them, with her attention on Louis and the Prefect. Now she realized that the man standing beside Mme. Masson had the same comfortable presence as the Prefect himself. Dr. Serge Michelin, the President of this fledgling university system, said, "Jean-Pierre, there shouldn't be any problem with Dr. Howard's name change. We're very excited about having her here."

"Merci, *Monsieur le President*," Bishou replied, "you are kind."

Next to him was the Humanities department chairman, which also hadn't registered. He wore a wry smile. "Nonetheless, I feel like the man who has had news broken to him by degrees, Professeur. First, I learned that you were not a man. Then, I learned that you were American. Now, I learn that you are to be married. And, I learn you plan to change your name! You have toyed with me." Dr. Rubin was almost teasing.

"I admit, I did toy with you a bit, Dr. Rubin," she said, smiling up into his face. "But I knew when we both spoke at the same time, stood at the same time, and shook hands at the same time, that we would get along well. This will be a very enjoyable place to work." Department heads lived for employees who spoke that way about them, so he was easily appeased.

"You are a brave man, Louis," said the Prefect seriously. "Many men would be unable to stagger back to their feet to fight again, as you have done."

"*Vous êtes très gentil, Monsieur le Prefect.*" Louis shook his head. "I have made a profound number of mistakes in but a few years. I am very fortunate to have the chance to put things right." Bishou, still holding his elbow, realized that he was very calm and realistic about the past. Their gazes met.

The Prefect saw. "Perhaps a little love matters, too," he observed. "You'll come to dinner some night, Louis, and we'll talk."

"I would be honored, Monsieur." Louis turned to escort Bishou in another direction, as the Prefect turned his attention to another conversation.

The head librarian introduced himself, and asked Bishou about getting a copy of her dissertation for their collection. She promised him one. They made small talk with various other people until, at last, Bishou said to Louis, "Are you ready to leave?"

"*Oui*, if you are."

They paid their respects to the librarian, the host of this event, and departed.

Outside, in the fresh air, Bishou said, "That wasn't so bad, was it?"

"*Embrace-moi,*" said Louis. She turned to him and put her arms around his neck. He wrapped his arms around her body. They kissed in the moonlight. "Non. This part, especially, is very good."

Gently, Bishou kissed him again. "You look so nice tonight."

"*Moi!* Regard her, this beauty, telling *me* I look nice. *Moi!*"

"Well." She kissed him again. "You do."

"*Allons.* Back to the car." They walked to the parking area, holding hands. Louis saw her into the car, got into the driver's seat, and drove out of the area.

He drove past the turn for her street. "Louis, you've missed the pension."

"I am taking you home," Louis said calmly and determinedly. She wasn't ready to fight about his definition of "home." Instead, she closed her eyes and enjoyed the ride.

"You are not arguing with me," Louis said.

"I don't want to argue with you," Bishou replied.

He reached over and stroked her leg. They were silent all the way to Rue Dessant. Louis was getting impatient, and she was weakening. Bishou didn't know what she was going to say to him if he tried to take her upstairs, to bed. Probably yes.

Then, they saw a car in the drive—an elderly gray Ford sedan. Puzzled, Bishou asked, "Whose car is that?"

"I know I've seen it before." Louis searched his memory. "Ah!" he said at last, "I know where I've seen it. At Garros."

"The airport? I don't understand."

"We have guests." Louis pulled up behind the gray car, and turned off the engine. His mood had changed. He hurried around the Mercedes, and opened Bishou's door. "Come in and say hello to them."

Bishou accompanied him to the house. She was surprised to see Louis open the door himself, rather than Bettina. Inside, they could hear voices from the kitchen, and laughter. The voices sounded familiar.

Louis led her to the kitchen and opened the door.

Bettina and Madeleine rose from the kitchen table, startled, smiles still on their lips. The man seated opposite them, with two boys eating a late supper, certainly needed no introduction.

"Oh, my Lord," said Bishou, in English. "Bat, you're here!"

Her brother stood, grinning. His eyes, as gray as hers, took in the nice clothes. "Wow." Then he held out his arms. They embraced. "Hello, little sister, we're here," said Jean-Baptiste 'Bat' Howard.

From the other side of the table, Andre and Gerard came around, too, for their hugs and kisses. Bat shook Louis's hand, but Louis reached out and hugged a younger boy with either arm. "Andy. Gerry." He had thought this out in advance, and had the right name for the right boy. "I am glad you could make it here. Welcome."

"Louis, it's good to meet you." Bat switched back to French, out of courtesy for the housekeepers.

"How did you get here?" Bishou asked.

"I told you, Garros."

"I recognized the rental car from the airport," Louis explained to her, "and realized the Howards had driven themselves here."

Bat nodded. "We got directions to Rue Dessant, then got here and found out you were gone. Good thing you'd told the ladies that we'd be staying upstairs, because I didn't know what the arrangements would be. *Merde*, Bishou, you look gorgeous. You didn't do this for a lecture, did you?"

"Non, non," said Louis, "we attended another reception afterward. But now, *tout le monde* knows the beautiful woman *professeur* at Université Français de l'Océan Indien. And her escort."

Bat grinned. "That is as it should be."

"Then come in to the salon with us," said Louis. "Bettina, some tea for Mademoiselle Bishou and me."

"Oui, monsieur," said the housekeeper happily, as Louis led the way out of the kitchen back to his own comfortable sofa. Bat took the easy chair while Louis pulled Bishou onto the couch beside him.

In answer to her questions, Bat replied, "We left Logan and flew to Orly, it seems like days ago. Then Orly to Garros. The boys were thrilled with all the foliage and the jungle animals. They could just wander around your backyard until dawn."

"But you look sleepy," she told the boys. "The *décalage* is finally getting to you. You need to try to sleep, even though your bodies say it is daytime."

"I'm not tired," protested Andy.

"Come," Bishou said, taking him in her arms. He leaned against her on the couch, while she leaned against Louis.

Bat commented to Louis, "I'll bet you didn't plan to take on an entire family."

"I will take that bet," said Louis good-naturedly. "They don't call you 'les jumeaux' for nothing. It is the whole family, not just you two."

"Well, that is true," Bat admitted. "Any two of us are 'the twins,' really."

"I have figured out that part," Louis replied, his arm around Bishou's shoulders.

Andy looked up at him, past Bishou. "What do we call you? You're even older than Bat. Calling you just 'Louis' doesn't seem right."

"The Campard boys call me Oncle Louis, and I'm not truly their uncle," Louis replied seriously. "Would you rather call me that, too, even though it is not quite accurate?"

Andy consulted Gerry, beside him on the couch, with a look, then looked back again at Louis. "Sure. That would be good."

"Bon. Oncle Louis it is, then." He drew Bishou closer. "And what do you think of your sister? A beautiful woman, *hein*? Did you ever notice before?"

"Not really." Andy nestled against her.

"But Bat said we'd see her differently now, because you did," Gerry contributed.

"Oh, he did," said Bishou. Bat grinned and said nothing. "Did he tell you I would always love you as much as I do?"

"Yes, he did," said Andy, eyes closed.

"Good," she said softly, kissing the top of his head. "I'm glad he realized that part. I will always love you."

"*Aussi*," said Louis, just as softly. "Now. Did Bettina show you the room upstairs where you boys will stay?"

"Yes. We took our suitcases up."

"Good. Now, Bat. You take them up and put them to bed, and come back to us."

"Yes, sir. Come on, boys."

After they left the room, Bishou said to Louis, "You are handling them just the right way. They need a commander-in-chief."

"I rather thought so. Besides, I am being selfish." Louis kissed her. He placed his hand under her breast, and kissed below her throat. In her ear, he said, "I may be acquiring your family, but you are *ma femme*."

She sighed, put her arms around his neck, and kissed him. "Oh, *mon mari*."

"What do you say?" he prompted with a smile.

"Ah, oui."

She slipped off her shoes and lay on the couch, her head in his lap. His hand rested on her breast and stomach.

"Go to sleep," he said. "I will get you back to the *pension*, I promise."

She closed her eyes.

Bettina's voice. "Is she asleep, monsieur?"

"Not yet," he replied. "But she had a very strenuous day, between teaching and this reception." She heard the clink of a teacup and saucer. "Merci. Leave the other here, in case she wakes." His tone changed. "What?"

"Oh, she is so beautiful, Monsieur. And kind. I am so happy for you."

"Oui. And kind. Now scat."

Bettina giggled. "Oui, Monsieur."

A few minutes later, she heard Bat sit down again in the other chair. "Is she asleep?"

"Oui."

"I'm glad. She's been overdoing it again."

"There are so many things she wants," said Louis.

"Not really," said Bat. "Only one thing she wanted. And she got him."

"You flatter me."

"Non," Bat insisted. "She wrote me months ago, from Virginia, and said, 'I have seen him, the only man I want.'"

"Really?"

"And listed all the reasons why there was no hope in hell of it happening."

Louis's hand stroked her body. "To think I never noticed her there, caught up as I was in my own problems."

"When did you decide she was the one?"

"Back here, without her. I argued with Etien. You know, I love the Campard family; they have stood by me through thick and thin. But whenever I mentioned my first wife's name, they suppressed me firmly. In Virginia, Bishou and the others let me mention Carola, and saw nothing wrong with it. She had been part of my life. I said her name here, thinking no more of it than that, and Etien grew angry. He told me I must not speak of her again. And damn it, no matter how horrible it became toward the end, there was a time that I loved her and she was my wife. I could have grown furious with him—but Bishou was at my shoulder, saying, non, non, he is your best friend, state your reasons for your anger. Work this through. And I did. I told Etien I was *un veuf*, I had a right to live as one. Bishou was there, saying, work this reasonably. We did. I realized I wanted her here, helping me with my life. I had begun wondering what I could do to bring her here, just my little dreams, when she showed up at the Campards' doorstep. Even she admits it was as if I summoned her." He stroked her hair. "Now, we are doing what other people have seen in us, all along."

"You could be right," said Bat.

Again, Louis stroked her hair. "I was—how to say it—badly burnt. *Une vierge trahisée.*" A virgin betrayed. So he knew that.

"Tough thing for a man to say," said Bat.

"Tough thing to live," Louis returned.

"Did you ever think about ending it, yourself?" Only Bat would dare ask.

"Oui, I did. But I think I have never completely given up hope. My dark days, I said, 'There must be more than this.'"

"I'm glad," said Bat. "That augurs good things for the future. Bishou could tell you of the miserable Viet vets washed up on our doorstep, asking for me, saying isn't there more than this, Sergeant-Major, I need something. Like me, she has always welcomed them with open arms. If they are asking, there is hope. The hopeless ones stay home and eventually kill themselves."

"I do understand, Bat. And you understand that there is a place here for you, too, and the boys. You now have a home on each side of the world." His weight shifted; apparently he and Bat had reached out and shaken hands.

Bishou shifted and moaned slightly. She sat up. "Mmph. I fell asleep."

"You must have needed it, *ma petite*," said Louis fondly. "You have had a busy day." He held her as she once held him, long ago in Virginia, half-asleep. He drew her against his body and reached for a cup. "Here. This tea is cool enough now." She sipped from the cup he held to her lips. "Still sleepy, *hein*?"

"*Oui*. I must go to bed."

"I will take you back to the pension."

Bishou sighed. "I might sleep until noon, now that the pressure is off."

Bat chuckled. "I'll bet you'll wake with the nine o'clock ferry."

"I always do," she admitted.

"I am the one who will be too excited to sleep," said Louis. "Even the boys with their *décalage*, they will pass out. They won't spend a restless night."

"We'll think up something to do tomorrow," Bat told him.

"Brother," Bishou threatened, "you will *not* bring him to

church on Friday morning, hung over. I will kick your ass from here to Paris if you do."

"No, ma'am," said Bat. Louis grinned. "We'll phone and leave a message what we're doing, once we get a plan. I'm thinking, a whole ocean, we ought to get out on it."

"Again, I remind you that alcohol and water don't mix, no more here than on a New England lake."

"Yes, ma'am." Bat lifted up a packet from the floor beside him. "By the way, this is for you. From our parents." He handed it across.

Puzzled, Bishou gently untied the string and opened the packet. There were two envelopes, and a tissue-wrapped package that contained a yard of white lace. "Why, this is from Maman's veil."

"Yeah!" Bat was equally surprised. "It's been in her bureau drawer for thirty years. Who would have thought she was saving it for her daughter's wedding?" He watched her examining the envelopes. "A letter from each of them?"

"Yes. Both marked 'Personal.'"

Bat smiled wryly. "And, I'll bet, both full of advice."

"Some of it good," she agreed. "I'll read them tonight."

"Come." Louis stood, and reached out a hand. "I'll take you home."

They were silent until they reached the pension. Louis shut off the engine, turned to her, and kissed her passionately. "This has been a good day," he murmured in her ear. "It lacks only one thing—my wife in my bed. If your brother hadn't been there, I think you might have stayed. Now we will never know, will we?"

She laughed quietly and kissed him again. "*Bonne nuit, mon amour.*"

"*Bonne nuit.*" Another kiss. "Let me get your dress bag from the trunk—although it seems foolish, for in another day, it will come to my house anyway."

"Then take it back with you," she replied. "I had forgotten about it. There's really nothing there I will need tomorrow."

"You are certain?"

"I am certain."

"All right." He got out of the car, came around, and opened her door. They walked to the front door of the pension.

Joseph opened the door. "Ah, *bonsoir*, mademoiselle, monsieur. I was just locking up."

"I'm here, Joseph." She turned and kissed Louis one last time, then went inside.

Joseph smiled as he barred the door. "You look very nice tonight, mam'selle."

"*Merci*, Joseph. It has been a long day. *Bonne nuit.*"

"*Bonne nuit*, mam'selle. Sleep well."

"Thank you, the same to you." She went upstairs to her room, changed into her pajamas, and washed up.

She got out the letters her parents had sent, and opened Dad's first.

"Ma chère Bishou," he wrote, "Jean-Baptiste has told us a very little about the man you will marry. Of course I am anxious—my little girl! You have taken many dares, but they have all been here in North America. Now I am watching you move to Africa, to a land I am told is as close to paradise on earth as one might find. But these visions might be deceitful—one does not know until one lives it.

"Oh, mon enfant, it was so good to have you here for so long, taking care of the boys while your brother was in the military. But even then, I thought, perhaps hoped, that someday you would want children of your own. I already know that you will be a good wife and mother, because I have seen you with the boys. You are patient, loving, and kind.

"Jean-Baptiste has not told me much about Louis, except that he is indeed the Louis Dessant of the Dessant Cigarette family.

He is wealthy and well-established. But I seem to recall there was some scandal in that family, so do be careful, ma cherie.

"My heart breaks to think that I might never see you again, but we live in hope. May God bless you and your good husband. With love, Dad."

Maman's letter was quite different.

"Chère Bishou, my little girl," she wrote, "You are young and strong, and not as cynical as your brother Jean-Baptiste, so I worry for you. You willingly go to a man's bed half a planet away, with no one to aid you if he should be cruel to you. I think Jean-Baptiste will stay long enough to make certain you are all right, but one never knows. If this man Louis is rich, he may also be intemperate and inconsiderate. Every man has only one way to show his love to a woman, he gives his body. Do not mistake love for physical passion! But if you give your soul to him, give also your body. To a man, that means so much more.

"I send my maman's lace to you, so that it may continue down through the women of our family. I hope for your greatest happiness. Write us. With love, Maman."

Maman certainly has her opinions on sex, Bishou thought. *It's lucky I wasn't there to listen to an entire lecture on the topic—it would have been uncomfortable.* She wondered when the last time her parents had made love, and suspected it was a long time ago.

With that thought, Bishou went to bed.

Chapter 6

In a way, Bat was right—Bishou woke up to the sound of the
ferry's horn. But then, she closed her eyes and fell asleep again.

She heard a *tap, tap* at her door, and hauled herself out of
bed to open it. It was Eliane, amused at her disheveled guest.
"Mademoiselle, you look exhausted."

"What time is it?"

"Almost eleven." The prim-looking elder sister held out a piece
of paper. "I have a message from your brother Jean-Baptiste. He
said to tell you the boys are at the Campards, and he and Louis
were going to East Beach. The Ford is in front, if you want to use
it today. You drive, I take it."

Bishou stared. "Bat stopped here?"

Eliane nodded. "What a handsome young man, your brother,
and so approachable! It was a pleasure to meet him." Yes, Bat had
captivated the hostesses.

"Is the car all right, in front?"

"Of course. Would you rather park it in back?"

"Yes, please. I don't need it for this morning's errands, probably
not until after lunch."

"Dress and wash up, then, and Joseph will show you the alley
to our back area. There's room to park it there." Eliane left.

Bishou washed up, and tried to clear the cobwebs from her
brain. She dressed, went downstairs, and found Joseph. He showed
her the alley and directed her through it to the little back areaway.
As was their custom, Bat had left the keys above the visor, but now
she placed them in her pocket. She locked the car. It would now
be out of sight and out of mind until she needed it later.

Bishou walked to Rue Marché, Market Street. Her first stop

was the jeweler; next was the florist. She saved her most time-consuming errand for last.

The Sundress Shop was having a busy morning. There were visitors, buying casual clothes for their vacation on Réunion Island. Madame Ross nodded to her, and finished with her current customers. When they left the store, Mme. Ross said, "Well, are you excited, Mademoiselle Bishou?"

"Very much. Is Ceci around?"

"Of course. Ceci!" Madame called to the back room. Ceci appeared, and nodded shyly at Bishou.

"I hope you don't mind," Bishou said apologetically. "But your hair is so much like mine—I wondered where you got it done."

"Er—Mma Jo's," Cecil replied, "*mais nous sommes noires.*" But we're black. "I straighten it, too."

Mme. Ross was smiling. "Mademoiselle Bishou's hair is naturally straight, but I can see what she means. She doesn't want a permanent, or oil treatment, or anything usually done in a French hair salon, do you, Mademoiselle?"

"Yes, that's it exactly. And, you see, I grew up with only brothers, and my mother has always been ill, so I haven't had a lot of advice. And your hair is so nice."

Mme. Ross explained to Bishou, "You must understand about Mama Josephine. She is hairdresser, sometimes barber, sometimes nurse midwife, whatever someone needs in her neighborhood."

"She sounds like a good person to know," said Bishou.

Mme. Ross's smile grew wider. "Ceci, why don't you take Bishou around to Mama Josephine's? It's a nice sunny day for a walk. Bishou can see her shop, and decide if it's right for her."

"Oui, Madame," said Ceci doubtfully.

As they walked along the sidewalk, Bishou said to Ceci, "I'm sorry to embarrass you. And it must be an embarrassment, to be seen with a white woman."

"Oh, non, mademoiselle, it's nothing. This is La Réunion, you know. And besides, you are *Americaine*."

"True," Bishou agreed good-humoredly. "I am forgiven many mistakes because I am *Americaine* and so I must not know any better."

Ceci giggled. "And you never will, will you?"

"Not if I can help it," Bishou concurred.

They were walking into a neighborhood that was obviously much darker than Rue Marché, but just as busy. "This is nice. These open-air markets remind me of Virginia, where I went to university."

"Really?"

"Yes. When visited the coast, we always went to the open-air markets, my friends and I." She thought fondly of Marie Norton, her friend and head resident of the EVU grad-school housing units, to whom she'd written a letter only yesterday.

Ceci led her to a building with a plate-glass window, through which Bishou could see the hoods and hoses of hair dryers. The front door was open. They stepped inside.

A well-endowed black woman spoke in French. "*Oui, madame?* May I help you?" Then she saw Ceci. "Ah, *bonjour, ma petite.*"

"Mma Jo, this is my friend Bishou. She said her hair is like mine. She wants to get it washed and trimmed."

"*Bonjour, madame,*" Bishou greeted her.

If Mama Jo was surprised to see a white customer enter her shop, she didn't show it. "Come sit down and let me look at your hair and scalp."

"*Oui, madame.*" Bishou sat down in the chair indicated by Mama Jo. The hairdresser then sat near her, and combed her hair.

"Smooth. Not washed too often."

"I hate washing my hair."

"You keep your natural oils, then. Too many women wash them all away. You just wash and cut, eh?"

"Bishou grew up in a houseful of brothers," said Ceci.

For the first time, Mama Jo chuckled. It was a warm sound. "And your heart brought you to Ceci, and Ceci brought you here. Let me see your hands."

Bishou gave her both hands, which she examined carefully. "You tend to your skin, but not your nails. You eat food that is good for you, and you drink water, but not quite enough."

"Ladies' restrooms are often difficult to find."

"Mmph. Is this pretty blue stone on an engagement ring?"

"Oui, madame."

Mama Jo deduced, "Then you are the tobacco-man's wife."

Bishou admitted, "Oui, that's me."

"Little fool," said Mama Jo, patting her hand, "you could have any beautician in the city, and she would come to your house."

"I would rather not have an expensive beautician. I would rather have a good one. And I am not a tiny little blonde Frenchwoman, and never will be. So why should I pretend?"

Now, Mama Jo's smile was wide. "And here is where the other girls come to make their skin whiter and their hair straighter."

"That is the other girls, not me."

"What does your man want?"

"My man wants someone to hold. He wants to be kissed and petted."

"He wants a woman," said Mama Jo.

"Oui, he wants a woman," Bishou replied, wondering exactly where this conversation was leading.

Mama Jo made a decision. "Come. I'll wash your hair, and trim it."

Bishou flung her purse and shopping bag behind a chair and followed her to the sink. Mama Jo wrapped Bishou's body in a neck-apron and tilted her back to wash her hair. The warm water made Bishou close her eyes and relax.

"You're not wearing makeup," said Mama Jo.

"I wanted to get my hair done," Bishou answered.

"Many women would not dare be seen without *maquilleur,* especially Frenchwomen."

"*Elle est Americaine,*" said Ceci, who waited nearby.

This startled Mama Jo. "*Americaine!* And you found your way to me?"

"*Oui, madame.*" Bishou kept her eyes shut. The shampoo and scalp massage felt so good. She hadn't realized how tense she was, either. The tension was now vanishing. She sighed, "Oh, I want to stay in this chair. I don't want to go back out into the world."

Mama Jo chuckled again. "Do you love your man?"

"I love him very much."

"Then I'll give you some massage oil for him, so he will feel like that, too."

"You are very kind."

"You will be lying with him for the first time?" Mama Jo asked.

"*Oui,*" Bishou admitted, blushing.

"Then I will give you a jar of cream, too, with lanolin in it, for your breasts and thighs, in case he is rough with you. Prison men are often rough," Mama Jo said frankly, "whether they mean to be or not."

"*Merci.* That is a good idea," said Bishou.

"How long was he in prison?"

"Seven years, at hard labor."

Mama Jo let out a silent whistle. "It seemed like a moment, to those of us who weren't there. I remember his wedding, to the first Madame Dessant."

"*Oui,* to Celie Bourjois, who was actually Carola Alese."

"Daunting, non? To be *la deuxième Madame Dessant?* Something to live up to?"

"*Non,* Mama Jo. On my worst days, I still treat him better than she did."

"*Oui,*" she said thoughtfully, toweling Bishou's hair. "I signed one of the petitions to the Prefect for his release."

"He and the Prefect are friends. The petitions were quite effective," said Bishou.

"That is nice to know, that something good came of them. Perhaps there is some justice in the world, after all." Mama Jo motioned Bishou to another chair. Bishou moved. Mama Jo took a razor, and began trimming the ends of Bishou's hair. "I remember that day. We went to the wedding—I think everyone did. We sat in the back. I saw the ring that did not fit until she forced it on, herself. I saw her face like stone. I said to Armand, '*Mon Dieu*, he is an innocent virgin, he will be sorry for this.' But surely, no one expected something like what happened."

Bishou smiled. "You are married to Armand, the bus driver?"

"*Oui*. How do you think I knew who you were?"

"*Bavardage*," Bishou grinned. Gossip.

Mama Jo chuckled, a deep chuckle that suited her. "There is enough of that, too. I am glad to confirm my gossip from the source, though."

"So far, you haven't been wrong about anything."

Ceci giggled, "Mama Jo is never wrong about anything."

"Hush, child!" Mama Jo chuckled, still trimming. "That is not true. But maybe we will come over and sit in the back. When are you married?"

"Tomorrow morning."

"And no plans for little ones yet?"

"I think that will just happen," Bishou replied.

"Madame is a teacher," said Ceci.

"You are? Will they let you teach if you're carrying a child?"

"It depends on how much they want me to teach, or how much I want to stay home."

"Well, you don't need the money, do you?"

Bishou sighed. "Yes and no. I don't always want to take and take and take from Louis, *comprendez-vous?* Like Carola did. Even Louis called her a parasite. If all I do is keep practicing my teaching, and cover my bus fare and café expenses, then I will be content."

"Maybe a *bonne* for the days you will not be with your children?" Mama Jo suggested.

"I cannot force myself to think that far ahead, but I suppose yes."

"You have strong muscles. You have a body that a man would want. I don't think it will be long before you are *enceinte*. You should plan for it."

"*Mon Dieu*, let me get through the wedding first."

This time, Mama Jo laughed outright.

She soaked Bishou's hands, and gave her a manicure. Then she soaked her feet, and gave her a pedicure. Bishou hadn't even thought about that—the open-toed shoes.

"Where are your parents, Bishou?"

"Back in America. They are too sick to travel so many thousands of kilometers. My father has a brain injury from a car accident. My mother is in a wheelchair, from the same accident."

"You have no family here?"

"*Non*, my elder brother Jean-Baptiste and my younger brothers Andre and Gerard are here. Today, Andy and Gerry are with friends, and Bat—Jean-Baptiste—has gone off somewhere with Louis."

"He will not bring him back sober," Mama Jo predicted.

"He had better, or find another continent to hide on. I already told him so."

Mama Jo chuckled. "They are men. They will do what they wish."

"Probably true," Bishou admitted.

Mama Jo applied a light polish to toenails as well as fingernails. "Hold still and let this dry."

"Oui, madame."

"I am simply not used to *une zoreil* calling me Madame."

"Then adjust to it," said Bishou, as frankly as Mama Jo had spoken to her.

"No. You will call me Mma Jo, as others do."

"As you wish," Bishou replied.

Bishou stood and gathered up her purse and shopping bag. Mama Jo added the massage oil and crème jar to her bag. At the front counter, Mama Jo named a price that was half what Bishou was used to. Bishou added a tip, and thanked her.

Ceci walked with Bishou back to Rue Marché. "Did I make you lose time from work?"

"*Un peu*. But it was interesting, and Madame Ross will want to know what happened."

"I like that place. I liked Mma Jo. I didn't realize, at first, that you were saying Mma Jo." Mrs. Joe.

Ceci nodded. "Or Mama Jo. We use either name for her, she doesn't mind."

"So I gathered. May I give you something, too?" She pulled out a ten-franc note and gave it to Ceci.

Ceci smiled like she had been given the keys of the kingdom. "Thank you so much, Mademoiselle Bishou—Madame Bishou."

"Thank you for your help," Bishou replied, and began the walk back to the pension.

Now she spent time cleaning out her hotel room. When the car contained everything but what she needed tomorrow, she trundled on to Rue Dessant. Bettina met her at the door.

"I've come to bring over my things," Bishou told her.

"For your new room upstairs, madame?" Bettina smiled.

"Oui, for that room."

She brought in backpacks, packages, notebooks, and clothing. Bettina helped her arrange things in a brown rattan-and-iron armoire that blended perfectly with the other furnishings of the exotic bedroom. They also turned the little desk in the salon, next to the telephone, into a work desk for Bishou. Currently it was idle, containing only a few bills Louis needed to pay.

"There," said Bishou at last, "I have everything out of the hotel room except the few things I will need tomorrow. I can make up one last bundle of those, or someone else can."

"There is not much here," Bettina said doubtfully.

"I'll send for my trunk from home, later. But, you know, much of what is in my trunk are clothes for the colder weather of New England. I don't really have much I want to bring to this new life."

Tears fell from the older woman's eyes. "'This new life.' Oh, if you knew what that meant to Monsieur Dessant. He says, 'I suggested Bishou buy a sundress here, she's never had one.' And he says it so quietly. But it makes him so happy."

"I want to make him happy," said Bishou. "He's such a good man. He really deserves happiness."

The tears were out of control. "He's like a little boy sometimes. I so—so don't want to see him hurt."

"We'll do our best to keep that from happening," Bishou promised.

*

With Denise riding shotgun and the boys in the back, Bishou drove the old gray Ford down the coast road. "So how far to East Beach?"

"Fifteen minutes, maybe twenty," Denise replied. "Do you know what they're up to?"

"Bat said something about getting out on the ocean, so I wouldn't be surprised if he rented a boat or a canoe."

"On the ocean!"

"They're both strong men," Bishou reminded her. "It's not as if you and I were going to do it."

"I should say not! I'm glad they didn't drag Etien along—Bat telephoned him and told him to mind the store because he was taking Louis."

"They have everything covered, don't they? Thank goodness for Etien." Bishou suspected that Etien was physically weaker than the other two, and parking him at the factory had been a good thing. But she would never hint as much.

At last they were at *Plage Est*, East Beach, a gravelly and sandy strip just off the grass. Louis's white car was parked there. They got out, and the boys went tearing down the beach, calling to each other.

"Oh, they'll get their clothes all wet and sandy!" Denise complained.

"Well, they are boys," Bishou returned. "We can't send them out naked, can we?"

"Speaking of boys." Denise touched her shoulder, and pointed out toward the Indian Ocean.

There were several boats out there, all canoes, rowboats, or similar styles. One caught her eye. It was canoe-like, running parallel to the shore, with two men paddling. Both were shirtless and intent upon their work.

Bishou tsked. "The Bodies Beautiful."

"But they *are* beautiful," said Denise.

They must have seen the women, because they turned to paddle in their direction. It was easy to see muscles strain on both competent oarsmen. At last, they were close enough to jump into the water and drag the boat in. Both men were barefoot and had rolled up their pants legs, but were seawater-soaked nonetheless.

Bishou kicked off her shoes, ran out, and grabbed hold of the canoe. It was a heavy one, vintage 1940 or 1950, but many hands made light work. They dragged it up onto the beach.

She knew Bat had stayed in shape, but had never really thought about what hard labor had done to Louis's body. His chest was every inch as well-muscled as that of the soldier. He concentrated on dragging the boat further aground, and then glanced up at Bishou with a smile.

"All right," said Bat, "I think that's where we got it from. Hey, baby sister." He reached into his pocket, unperturbed, pulled out a waterproof packet, and freed a cigarette and matches from it. In a moment he was smoking, walking back to Denise with them. The men opened the trunk of Louis' car and got their clothes out.

"Where are the boys?" asked Louis. The women pointed down the beach, where they had already found some other children to play with.

"Mmph, good," approved Bat. "Fresh air and exercise."

Louis pulled a blanket out of the trunk. "I'm going to sit down for a while and dry off. *Viens, cherie.*"

Bat reached out his hand. Bishou placed the keys to the Ford in it. Bat told her, "You stay with Louis. I'm going to go back with Denise and everyone, and get ready to play Boy Scouts tomorrow night."

"How so?"

"We're going to have a tent in Campards' back yard the night of the wedding—it was okay with Etien. The boys are going to sleep outside, cook their own meal—I'm going to pick up ingredients for macaroni and cheese—and just hang out."

"Very considerate of you, Sergeant-Major," said Bishou.

Bat grinned. "You can return the favor someday." Rather than don his shirt, he draped it over his shoulder, and barked, "*Allons-y, mes garçons! Allons-y!*"

"Put on your shirt," Bishou directed. "Madame Campard is a respectable woman. You must not embarrass her." He obeyed, and buttoned up.

"*Milles pardons, madame,*" he said, the cigarette still not budging between his lips. Then he grinned, and ambled off to the Ford with Denise, the boys in his wake.

Louis laughed. He carried the blanket back out to a grassy spot, and spread it. He lay down, his shirt open, and let the sun and the wind dry him off. Bishou sat down beside him. His cheeks and chest were tinged with red, sunburn or windburn, but with the promise of health.

Louis folded his arms behind his head, still happy. "This was a good day. I will sleep well tonight, after all."

"I'm glad."

He stroked her leg. "You are not wearing stockings."

"I'm wearing sandals today."

"Ah. I see. *Viens.*" He reached out for her.

Bishou lay down, her head on his shoulder and one hand on his bare, muscular chest. She felt the warmth of his chest, its rise and fall as he breathed. They remained that way for a long time.

"I rather like Bat," said Louis at last. "We have had some talks. He quite frankly asked me if you and I already slept together."

"I had already told him to mind his own business." She stroked his chest.

"Mm, *oui.* I told him I was a lonely, half-crazed widower, and not to judge by me. Then—I did tell him some of the things Carola did to me."

"I imagine that was pretty nasty," said Bishou.

"It was. As I told you, she taught me how to seduce and be seduced. She taught me sex. At the very end, she taught me love, misery, and death—all at the same time. Bat did say one wise thing—that I needed to be able to distinguish one from another."

"Well, that much is truth."

"I can distinguish them, Bishou. That I promise you."

She smiled, and stroked his chest again. "I think you can."

After a while, Louis announced that he was dry enough. He sat up and buttoned his shirt. Once in the car, they sought out the fisherman's café they had dined in on Sunday. What they wore didn't matter in this place. Today's catch was haddock, and it was good. They spoke mainly about the food and wine, because there really wasn't much else to say.

On the way home, he found a place to pull the car over. He

kissed her like he meant it, and opened his collar so she could kiss his neck and throat. Every movement was full of promise. *One more day*, she thought.

At last, he pulled back onto the road and drove her back to the pension. As he escorted her from the car to the hotel door, he held her hand. At the door, Louis placed her hand on his bare throat. With her other hand, she stroked his hair. He kissed the hand he had placed on his throat, and sighed. "And you cannot come home with me, because the clothes are here."

"Sleep, *mon ange*. I'll see you in the morning." She kissed him.

Louis looked unhappy. "This is so difficult."

"Shh, *non*, don't think so. Go home and sleep."

He wrapped his arms around her and held her tightly. "Bishou, I want you with me!"

"Shh, *mon treasor*, go home and sleep. Tomorrow will be here soon enough." Bishou kissed his lips again. "*Bonne nuit.*"

"*Bonne nuit*, ma Bishou." It took almost a physical effort for him to leave her and get back in the car.

Bishou thought of her mother's words, *the man gives you his body*. Maman had been right enough. She had felt it tonight.

Bishou noticed that it was barely sunset, but didn't care. She washed up, changed into her pajamas, and fell asleep.

Chapter 7

Bishou woke up to the jangling of her little alarm clock. She shut it off, climbed out of bed, and made a visit to the bathroom at the other end of the hall. Her hair brushed into place easily, and makeup could wait. This wasn't an ordinary day.

She opened the closet door. The dress still took her breath away, so she imagined the effect it would have on other people. It was made of white satin-cotton fabric with the barely visible swirls in it, and a lightweight lace train attached that could be swept up conveniently behind and buttoned in place almost one-handed by the bride herself. Nadine had definitely caught on to the fact that Bishou was a utilitarian bride.

She donned the sexy underwear, new garter belt, new stockings, and the pretty high heels. She was working the dress over her head when there was a tap at the door. Bishou pulled the dress down in place and called, "*Entrez!*"

Denise Campard wore a pretty knee-length blue dress, and a nice little pair of heels. "How are you doing?" She helped Bishou with the dress and hooked it shut. Bishou still wished heartily that French dresses had zippers.

"How do I look?" asked Bishou, regarding herself in the mirror.

"So far, so good," Denise answered with a smile.

Bishou sat down so Denise could brush out her hair and help with makeup. Denise applied it ably, although she admitted she never wore it herself. "But it's fun to dress up someone else," she concluded with a smile, using a lip-brush on Bishou. "You have such beautiful full lips, Bishou, a lot of cosmetics would be wasted on you. Just be natural."

"Usually, I am natural," Bishou replied. "Except for powder and lipstick, and I admit, more makeup when I go out in the evening. I want this to be just right, though—it needs a colder eye than mine."

Denise laughed. "I am glad you are taking such pains over it, because I want Louis to be happy almost as much as you do."

"I know, *ma soeur*," Bishou said fondly, patting her hand. Then she stood up suddenly. "Oh, oh, I knew I was forgetting something."

"Bishou! Taking care of you is my job. I am your attendant, remember?" Denise scolded.

Bishou only laughed, and reached toward the end table. She held up a jewelry box. "This is for you, Denise, your bridesmaid's gift."

"What—?" Denise stared as Bishou opened the box. Inside was a little silver charm bracelet, with two charms: a little blue stone and a silver square shaped like a cigarette box. The familiar stripe ran diagonally across the box, and in tiny letters it read DESSANT. Denise stared in wonder. "Bishou—it's beautiful. Thank you so much."

Bishou opened up the second box, and removed a matching bracelet. "As you put more charms on, yours will differ from mine, but today, they are the same." She slipped it on her right wrist.

"I am amazed you did this, on top of all the other things you've done in the past week," Denise said. Then she shook her head. "But no, you've been raising boys and getting a third college degree in your extra time, haven't you? So I guess I shouldn't be surprised." Denise, too, slipped on her bracelet, and clasped it in place. "Now. Sit down and let me pin your hat and veil in place."

"Who's driving us there?"

"Bat. I understand he had both boys cleaning the sea sand out of the rental car this morning, so there would be nothing left to soil a white dress."

"Nothing the Sergeant-Major does can surprise me anymore," Bishou said wryly.

"Oh, oui. When Etien telephoned this morning, it was Bat who answered. He completely threw Etien off when he said, 'Dessant residence.' For a moment, he wondered where on earth Louis had recruited a butler. Oh, be still. I can't pin this on while you're laughing that hard."

"I'm sorry," said Bishou. "No, I'm not."

Denise laughed, too. She finished her task. Now she herded her charge down the stairs.

To Bishou's astonishment, the lobby was full of people, who all oohed and aahed at her. The pension ladies were there, and Joseph, and the kitchen and cleaning staff, as well as Bat himself, dressed in his finest black-tie suit. He wore a white boutonniere. Bat regarded her approvingly. "Something old—"

She touched the lace train. "Maman's lace is sewn in there, too."

"Something new—"

"The dress and shoes."

"Something borrowed—"

"I'll send Maman's lace back with you."

"Something blue."

She held out her engagement ring.

Bat knelt. "And a sixpence for your shoe. Hold still, I've got a bit of wire, to wire it in place."

"Is that an old American wedding tradition?" Marie asked.

"Oui."

"Mademoiselle Bishou, you look so lovely," Eliane said.

Bat stood up. "*Prêt, ma soeur?*" Ready, my sister?

"*Prêt,*" Bishou replied. Bat held open the door, and the women stepped outside. There were more people on the sidewalk, admiring them as Bat opened the rear door for them. Their bouquets awaited them on the car seat. Bat closed their door, slid into the front seat, started the car, and began driving toward the church.

"We'll probably see most of those onlookers there," Bat

commented to his passengers in the back seat. "The church is a public place, and Louis is well-known."

"Oui," said Denise. "That is much as it was the last time."

"I hope he doesn't have any flashbacks," said Bat.

"Me too," Bishou said. "I'm more worried about that than anything else."

"We will be careful," Denise promised.

It felt like an eternity before they reached the church, only a few blocks away. Bishou recognized Louis's and Etien's automobiles. Bat pulled in beside them. Bishou waited for him to open her car door, but even that short delay was torture. Denise slid out the other door by herself.

Gerry and Andy waited outside the front entrance. They, too, stared at their sister as she climbed up the steps. In turn, she stared at them. "Wow," she told them. "You both look as handsome as Bat does."

The boys grinned. Gerry reported to Bat. "We came out here when Louis and Mr. Campard came onto the altar with the priest, just like we were supposed to."

"Okay," Bat prompted. "Now what do you do?"

"Sneak up the stairs and tell the organist to start playing."

"Quietly," he ordered. Bishou grinned as they took off like shots and did their best to tiptoe up the balcony stairs.

Bishou reached back and let the lace train drop to the ground. Denise fussed with it for a moment, spreading it out behind her.

Bat held out an elbow. It looked like he had taken a lesson from Louis on this. Bishou slid her hand under his arm, holding her bouquet firmly with the other, and said to Denise, "Are we ready?"

"We are ready," Denise replied, adjusting her own blue veil, shifting her small blue bouquet in her hands, and stepping in front of them. "If you faint or fall, *jumeaux*, I won't know until I hear the thud. So hiss if I need to stop. Otherwise, a stately step to the altar."

"Oui, madame," the twins chorused, and they grinned.

Denise led the way, with as stately a step as she promised. Père Reynaud stood with Louis and Etien. Denise stepped to one side as Bat and Bishou kissed. Then Bat placed Bishou's hand in Louis', and stepped back to the first pew. Louis brought her to the priest, and the ceremony began.

They had agreed to a full Mass as part of the ceremony. Bishou had wanted it for an additional reason. The Mass, its marriage readings, and the full ceremony progressed, as the bride and groom and attendants knelt and sat at the appropriate times. When they knelt for communion, the Campards received theirs first, then Bishou. She turned to watch Louis receive communion for the first time in ten years, with special dispensation. He was willing to pay his dues. Bishou might have cried if she hadn't heard Denise stifle a sob.

They stood before the congregation to exchange rings. That had been a conscious decision on their part, because Louis and Carola had knelt. First Bishou repeated her vow to love, honor, and obey, and slid the wedding band on Louis's finger. Then it was Louis's turn. He said the words, to love and honor, and she heard the quaver in his voice. He lifted up the ring, and almost dropped it. But Père Reynaud was on the alert, too. He grasped Louis's hands firmly as he realized how bad his tremors had become.

So did Bishou, as Louis reached for her hand to slip on the ring. Here was where the ring had not fitted Carola's finger, and Carola had taken it herself and forced it on—which should have been one of their first clues that she was not the intended.

Louis felt the pressure of their hands. And a third: Etien Campard placed his hand on Louis's shoulder at that moment. Bishou realized also that Denise stood beside her. If that ring hit the floor, she would pounce on it like lightning.

Louis Dessant's face changed. His brown eyes lit up. He smiled. At Etien, at the priest, at Denise, and last of all, he smiled into Bishou's eyes. Love and support—that was what he had now, like never before. Louis slipped the ring on her finger easily and repeated the wedding vow at Père Reynaud's prompting.

At last, Père Reynaud turned them toward the congregation, and announced, "Ladies and gentlemen, allow me to present Monsieur et Madame Louis Dessant." The congregation burst into applause. The organ music swelled. They walked swiftly down the aisle together, and back outside, where another crowd of *réunionnaises* awaited them, all the locals.

"Throw that bouquet," Louis advised, laughing. Bishou pitched it into the crowd amid squeals of delight. Photographers took candid pictures.

"What a pitch!" Etien exclaimed. "What sport do you play?"

Bat was there, too. "Hey, Denise, do you want yours, or will you give it to Bishou to pitch, too?"

"I want mine," Denise replied, laughing. "Don't touch me."

Louis laughed, sounding like himself. "*Viens, ma femme*, into the car," he said, taking her hand. She gathered up the lace train with her other hand, and ran with him to the white Mercedes. Mercifully, no one had gimmicked it up, perhaps feeling that it would be too cruel a trick on Louis's sensibilities. The Campards quickly followed them out of town, with the gray Ford behind that. Walkers, cyclists, and rickety vehicles straggled after them.

Bettina, Madeleine, and a squad of caterers were waiting in the Dessant front yard. The wedding table was festooned with flowers. A silver ice bucket containing champagne bottles waited near the table.

The wedding guests found their places at the table, if they had been part of the original plan, or set up picnic cloths and neighboring patio tables and chairs if they were add-ons to the party. The Howard boys and the Campard boys made themselves a backyard fort where they brought their own food and drink. There were people everywhere, eating and drinking and laughing.

Louis hadn't done this the first time around, either. They had just got married and gone home. There had been no family.

Bat and Etien laughingly opened champagne bottles, and distributed drinks. Then Etien toasted the new couple. *"Monsieur et Madame Dessant, a votre sante, et toute nos felicitations. Fait heureux."* Be happy.

"Brief and to the point," said Bat, toasting them also. "Mine is in the form of a threat. Make my baby sister unhappy, and I will be back here to deal with it, because I know where you live."

"Oui, Sergeant-Major," Louis laughed, entwining goblets with his wife. They sipped from each other's glasses long enough for the photographer to get another photo.

Bishou dug into the chicken marsala, salad, and rice. "I didn't realize how hungry I was."

"Nor I." Louis ate, too. "I didn't realize how my appetite had been affected."

"*We* did, Monsieur," murmured Bettina behind him. He turned and smiled at her.

"A good staff is a blessing beyond measure," he said, and both Bettina and Madeleine blushed. "Merci, you two."

Bishou leaned over and whispered in his ear, "Did we give them a gift?"

"This morning," he murmured. "White silk handkerchiefs."

"Whew."

Louis looked in his new wife's eyes, four inches from his, and smiled. "My companion, I had not forgotten." He looked pleasantly surprised as she leaned forward, champagne glass still in hand, and kissed him.

They walked around to the picnic blankets. One large blanket party were Creoles. There were Dessant Cigarette employees, and also Mama Jo and Papa Armand. Louis asked Mama Jo for a kiss, saying it was good luck; she told him no, he must kiss her. And he did. He also kissed the hands of both his secretaries, at another picnic blanket, and personally made sure their glasses were full of champagne. Nadine and Mme. Ross were there, too; Louis made certain they had champagne as well. Louis and Bishou made the full circuit, and Bat covered anyone they might have missed.

Claire Aucoeur stood before Bishou, and handed her a package. "Pardon, Madame Dessant, but I know this is something you wanted. I was able to get you a copy."

Bishou smiled, knowing what it must be as she pulled off the ties. Louis, coming over while she unwrapped it, asked, "What is that?"

"Claire remembered that I wanted a photograph of someone I loved," Bishou explained.

Louis frowned, puzzled, and pulled the framed photo out of the wrapper. He was stunned by whose picture it was. "You two!"

Bishou gazed again fondly at the promotional photography of Louis Dessant, taken for the business. "I shall cherish this. Thank you, Mademoiselle."

"My pleasure, Madame Bishou."

Louis and Bishou were crossing back to the table when they saw a convertible coming up Rue Dessant. Who was coming late, in casual clothes?

"Oh, *merde*," said Louis, as it stopped behind the other cars, and two couples emerged. He had recognized the vehicle, and the man driving. It was the Prefect.

"Oh, my God," muttered Bishou, and they walked toward the car.

Monsieur and Madame Masson were laughing. The other couple looked as if they were in on the joke, but weren't quite sure it would be taken well.

"Oh, *mon Dieu!*" said Bishou delightedly, loud enough to be heard. "*Monsieur le Prefect!*" She gave him the bride's kiss.

Louis' parole officer laughed. "Forgive us for crashing your party, Madame."

"Forgive you!" Louis exclaimed. "The least I can do is offer you some refreshment. Come, join us!"

"Allow me to introduce Monsieur et Madame Herriman," said the Prefect, as Bishou clasped his arm.

"Oh, my word," she said in English. "Welcome to the Dessant home, Monsieur l'Ambassador."

The American Ambassador smiled, and replied in English, "Thank you. Jean-Pierre said you wouldn't mind us dropping in, but we don't want to wear out our welcome."

"If you don't mind a yard full of people, some cake, and some champagne, you cannot possibly wear out your welcome," Bishou replied. She saw Louis offering his own arm to Mme. Herriman.

"Come," he said. "Join our celebration today. You are most welcome." Louis smiled down into her face. Mme. Herriman's smile showed that she was obviously taken with the attractive bridegroom.

There was some hurried bowing and scraping, and place-setting. Bat poured champagne for them while he asked how things were in Washington. They had cake and champagne and coffee, a nice little picnic-stop for their day out.

"We'd thought about stopping by the church," said Mme. Masson, "but we weren't really dressed for it. Then Jean-Pierre suggested we just stop by the reception."

"That was a wise move, if you are spending a day just relaxing," Louis agreed.

"I have been trying to tell the Herrimans that's what Île de la Reunion is all about, vacationing," said the Prefect. "It's one of our strengths."

"Bishou, you look lovely. That white dress is much like your blue one, isn't it?" asked Mme. Masson.

"Merci. Yes, it is. Both are by Madame Nadine, whom you must know."

"Ah, Nadine! Is she here? Ah, yes, she is! Excuse me, I'm going to say hello to her." Madame left them for the chairs where Nadine and Mme. Ross sat.

"I can't remember the last time I saw my wife this relaxed at a social event," the Prefect marveled. "This is a pleasant little party. You were wise to arrange it so, Louis."

"And so was Madame," Louis demurred. "We did not want the formality."

"I see a goodly cross-section of Saint-Denis here."

Bishou laughed. "Well, I have met a goodly cross-section of Saint-Denis."

"President Michelin told me he had been in touch with the President of East Virginia University—Lanthier, I think the name was?"

"Yes, President Lanthier."

"Who told him if he could snag Bishou Howard for his staff, do it. He suggested, too, that you might be willing to move into Administration, that you thought like an administrator, and had helped him a great deal."

Louis laughed heartily. He told them about the tobacco genetics bet he had made with other World Tobacco Conference attendees in Virginia. Bat, who had not heard this tale, grinned broadly as Louis described setting up Bishou for a talk about phenotypes and genotypes, and the thousands of dollars she netted for the college scholarship fund. Bishou blushed, while the Prefect roared with laughter.

"My dear girl, don't be embarrassed while these men sing your praises. A husband who brags about you, and the President of your last educational institution advising us to hang on to you! You are a fortunate woman." The Prefect glanced at Bat. "And your twin as well. I am ahead of the game. I don't think the others have met your twin brother, or even know you have one."

"Most of the time, we are on opposite sides of the world," said Bat.

"And still, you are *sympathetique, n'est-ce pas?*"

"Well, somewhat," said Bishou. Hard to explain, on the spot, that they weren't birth-twins, they just thought alike.

"We have worked well together," said Bat. "Now it's Louis's turn."

Louis shook his head. "Non, non, Sergeant-Major, I never take your place, I merely supplement it."

"We'll see in five years," Bat said agreeably.

"Sergeant-major," said the Ambassador alertly. "Marines?"

"Veteran, sir," said Bat. "Vietnam."

"And you won't be staying here. Reserves?"

"No, sir, retired. My family needed me."

"Hm," said the Ambassador, in a tone sounding suspiciously like "we'll see." *A Marine who spoke native French,* Bishou reflected, *would be a desirable acquisition.*

Mme. Masson returned with Nadine, who asked Bishou to stand up and show off her dress. Bishou obliged, while the two women talked fabrics and styles. Something about her dress, Bishou wasn't exactly sure what, was cutting-edge fashion. Bishou modeled, while other women came over to join the fashion group.

Then there were presents to unwrap. Bishou kept Louis's photograph near her. Bettina and Madeleine got the unwrapped gifts indoors, for later sorting and thanks.

Bishou realized in surprise that the caterers were beginning to pack up, and the sun was setting. The Prefect and his guests took their leave. Bat gathered up the boys and left for Rue Calaincourt. Other guests said their goodbyes and also left.

Denise and Etien were the last to go. Louis shook his friend's hand. "Much different this time, eh, *mon ami?*"

"Much different," Etien confirmed, clapping Louis's shoulder. "Great happiness to you both." He kissed Bishou. Denise kissed them both. Then they, too, left.

The caterers were taking down the last of the tablecloths, and folding up the tables and chairs. Louis took his wife's hand and entered the house.

The brandy and a few little silver things were in the living room. Most likely, the rest were back in the kitchen and pantry area, at least until tomorrow. There was room to sit down. Bishou moved to enter the room, but Louis caught her arm.

"Let's go upstairs," he said, in a husky voice.

"All right," she answered docilely. She was conscious of him behind her as she climbed the first flight of stairs, then the second. He reached past her to open the door of their bedroom. The taste of champagne stayed with Bishou. They had their own little bathroom, just like the room below; quickly she rinsed away the champagne taste.

Louis turned on the lamp near the bed and closed the door. He opened a wardrobe door and nodded approvingly at his clothes. Bishou unpinned her hat and set it on top of her armoire, and turned to watch him pull out his nightclothes, conventional husbandly pajamas.

"Don't wear the pajama top," she suggested.

Louis glanced at her. "As you wish." He removed his black-and-whites, hanging them up in the wardrobe. He flashed a quick smile at her. "You cannot unhook that by yourself, can you?"

"Probably, if I struggle with it."

"Don't struggle. I will unhook it. Give me a moment to change and wash up."

Bishou moved to the window. The view here was pleasant. Long shadows fell across the land as evening arrived. The full moon, too, had risen.

"Now. Come here," said Louis.

Bishou came and turned her back to him. He unhooked the dress and slid it up over her head. He tossed it on the bedroom chair. Immediately, he unhooked her brassiere as well, and tossed it with the dress. Then he sat on the bed and drew her toward him.

Bishou felt her pulse race and her breath change as he kissed her breasts and stomach. She made a small noise.

"What do you say?" he prompted, in a low voice.

"Ah, oui," she gasped, and he smiled.

It was the beginning of a night of loving and learning. Louis knew exactly what he wanted, and what she should feel. He proved beyond doubt that he had been the husband of an extremely sexually advanced woman, and that she had taught him well. He turned Bishou inside-out. He taught her what sounds to make, how to move her body, what to say and do, as they made love. The fireworks did not diminish. He moaned and whispered in her ear. He kissed and bit her body. Bishou had never felt anything like this. She couldn't have imagined it.

Finally, both were satisfied. She gasped when their bodies separated and Louis slid over beside her. "Sleep, *ma femme*," he said softly.

"Oui, *mon mari*," she responded, and closed her eyes.

Chapter 8

The sun shone on Bishou's face and woke her up. She felt Louis's hand on her chest before she opened her eyes. Louis was lying beside her, also naked, a sheet covering his hips and hers. He was propped on his right elbow, looking down at her. His left hand stroked a line down the middle of her chest. He wore his new wedding band on his ring finger, but also her class ring with the blue stone on his smallest finger.

Bishou heard the horn of the *Mauritius Pride* in the distance. "Mm. The ferry. I am so used to hearing that every morning, now."

"That is a sound of Île de La Réunion," he murmured, smiling. "You are *réunionnaise*, Madame." He stroked her. "I am sorry I was a little—rough on you last night. I was *fou d'amour.*" Mad with love.

"I would have wondered if you weren't, *mon mari*," Bishou replied.

Louis did not laugh. His half-smile remained. *He's peaceful*, she realized. *He's contented.*

"Are you happy, *mon amour*?" she asked him gently.

"*Oui.* A little afraid to be so happy."

Bishou smiled in understanding. "Because it cannot possibly last?" He was silent; his fingers stroked a line down her chest and stomach again and again.

At last Louis said, "I watched you sleep, and thought, how can I even bear to leave this room?"

"We will leave it together," she replied. "When you go to work, I will be here when you get home, or you will know where to find me. Always. I promise."

Louis bent down to kiss her lips, realizing that she understood his fear of desertion. Carola, the false wife, ditched him when she got her name on the bank accounts, and left with his fortune. Bishou returned his kisses. They lay in the bed, holding and stroking each other.

Louis murmured, "It is Saturday. No work awaits us. We have the day to waste as we wish."

"I know," she said. He smiled and kissed her again.

*

Bishou took a leisurely bath in the tub downstairs, while Louis slept in bed. He started his penance, too, for the packet the priest had given him was open on the bed when she came back up a flight to dress. He examined its contents.

The sun shone in the balcony window, lighting up the bedroom. While Bishou brushed her hair at the bureau, she turned to regard her husband, still in bed. He lay on his stomach, propped up on his elbows to read the little book. His chest, back and arms were bare, his shoulder muscles very visible at this angle. The cotton bedspread covered him from the hips down. *My God,* she thought, *what a beautiful man. To think that Carola wasted this.*

"Hm?" His head turned as she sat on the edge of the bed.

She slid the bedspread down to bare his back and hips. Bishou reached for the oil. "Lie down." He obeyed, looking a little wary. She poured a little of the oil from Mama Jo on her hands, and rubbed it into the smooth, warm skin of his back.

Louis closed his eyes and half-moaned, half-sighed. "That feels so good."

"It does to me, too, to my hands."

He said nothing. There was a smile on his lips. Yes, he was seductive.

She kissed his neck. Softly, he said her name. "*Oui?*" she said equally softly.

"What are you doing to me?" he murmured.

"Stroking you. You have a beautiful body." She still spoke softly in his ear, then kissed his neck and shoulders.

"Ah, *oui*," he sighed in pleasure.

"Ah, *oui?*"

"Ah, *oui, ma femme.*"

She rubbed oil into his lower back, his hips, then along his inner leg. He was startled by her touch. He rolled onto his back, naked, and reached out to her.

"*Viens.*"

She slipped off her robe and lay down. He wrapped her in his arms. They kissed and kissed. This was her siren, her man to pet and love. She abandoned any plans she might have made for the day, just to love him.

Bishou fell asleep, and woke hungry. Her movement, still in his arms, woke him. "Hm?"

"We need breakfast. Or lunch. Or, at this rate, dinner."

"I suppose so." Louis stroked her and sighed. "But I don't want to leave this island. It's peaceful."

Bishou understood that he meant the island of this bed, but she replied, "It is your island."

Louis smiled at the reference to Dessant Cigarettes, and sat up. She changed into day clothes as he did. They climbed downstairs, knowing their footsteps would be heard in the kitchen.

Sure enough, Bettina and Madeleine were quickly setting the table as they reached the bottom floor. "You have more warning, you two, with us on the top floor," Louis joked.

"Oui, but it is your honeymoon," the women replied, laughing, "take as long as you like, Madame et Monsieur."

"Our honeymoon. It is, isn't it?" Bishou mused, seating herself and pouring coffee for Louis, as the women went back into the kitchen for the food. "Strange. I had been so focused on the wedding, I hadn't even thought about the honeymoon."

"Even though I gave you that nightgown, and you bought sexy underwear?" Louis's brown eyes twinkled over the top of his coffee cup.

"Even though."

"*On dit*, they say, that honeymoons started out when a man seized a woman and carried her away from her family, then only fed her drugged honey for a month. Until she submitted willingly, or was carrying a child."

"Look." Bishou glanced at the coffee setting. "Honey. Do you want some in your coffee?"

"Oh, get away," Louis chuckled. "And I am already drugged, to feel this good."

"Well—if this is our honeymoon—" she began tentatively.

"Oui?"

"A ride on the coast road? That fisherman's café again?"

"A blanket in the grass?" he bargained in return. "You in a sundress?"

"We're guaranteed to run into the tour bus."

"Or Bat," Louis sighed. "I took him to that café. He said no wonder you liked it. You are twins, a year notwithstanding. Twins in thought and action."

"Pretty obvious, isn't it?" she agreed. "But that just makes him easy to please. We know what to expect."

"He needs a woman," said Louis.

"I know. He'll find one. Heaven knows who, or how, but Bat is resourceful."

"So are you." Louis paused. "He told me about the letter you sent him. Last spring. I don't think he expected to see tears in my eyes— because there were tears in his, too. Two grown men, sitting in a café, talking about a letter that wasn't even a love letter. A list of all the reasons why you dare not love me." He lifted her hand and kissed it.

"A real waste of ink, wasn't it?" Bishou said softly. "Bat knew at once that I'd fallen in love."

Gently, Louis kissed her hand again. "With a man growling at *larves de tabac*."

"With a working, thinking man who also happened to be very attractive—and a bit of a mystery," Bishou admitted.

"Am I still a mystery?"

"Parts of you."

Louis smiled, and stroked her hand. "And, of course, you are not."

"I'm pretty straightforward, I guess." They released hands to return to the coffee. Bettina reappeared with food. "I think I'd be afraid to keep a secret from you, Louis."

"How do you mean? Because of Carola?"

There was a *clack* as Bettina recovered a dish she almost dropped. How could she help but overhear such things discussed in this house?

"Oui, because of Carola. I know you said you don't like surprises. Now I know why. It will be difficult even getting you a Christmas present. You would be in a sweat of fear that I was buying a secret ticket to Japan."

Louis laughed. Without meaning to, Bettina giggled, too. Bishou turned and clasped her hand for just a moment. Bettina squeezed it, and went back to the kitchen.

Louis had seen the hand-clasp, and said, "I'm glad you get along well with my *domestiques*. Don't try to keep secrets from them, either. And as for me—there may be things I forget to tell you, but I promise you, no secrets."

She nodded. "At least, no unpleasant ones."

*

Louis and Bishou went for a drive, along the coast road. As he drove, Louis asked her, "Are you all right?"

"Me? Yes, I'm fine."

"You don't hurt, *ma Bishou?*"

"Well, *un peu.* Mama Jo gave me cream she said I would need. It is soothing. She also gave me the massage oil I used on your back."

"They say Mama Jo is a witch-woman."

"Maybe she is. Maybe we need one."

Louis grinned. "You sound so *réunionnais.*"

"My husband is *réunionnais.* I follow him."

The expression on his face changed. Louis drove in silence for some time. Then he asked, "Are you ready for church tomorrow?"

"Why not?"

"Does it bother you that I am a convicted felon?"

Bishou glanced at him in surprise. "Louis! Did you think this was news to me? I seem to recall reading a newspaper article about you." Now there was an understatement. That inflammatory *Paris Gazette* article had started all of this, in Virginia.

"Non, non. That is not what I meant."

"What did you mean, then?"

Louis pulled the car over on a grassy inland margin, shut off the engine, and turned to her. "I meant—I have lost many privileges. I cannot vote or partake in local politics. I cannot travel without permission. I can't even touch a gun. I must pay a lawyer to sign legal papers for the business, or ask Etien to do it alone. And— when articles like that *Gazette* one, about my fall, are reprinted—I pay for my crimes all over again."

"Louis." Bishou shook her head. "Neither of us can change that. It is part of being Louis Dessant. I am sorry that it bothers you. But I know that the Prefect also sees that it bothers you, and that you are contrite. Père Reynaud now knows, too. You learned from your mistakes, and now you value your friends and acquaintances more. Very few friends complain about being valued. And the *réunionnaises* I meet consider you part of them. Some of them have made some bad mistakes, too."

Louis smiled at the turn of phrase, aware that she must have heard it from someone acquainted with prison. "And you are willing to take me as I am."

"Why not? You were willing to take me as I am."

"Oh, no," he said. "I have done my best to make you into my wife and mistress."

"Well, are you not my husband and master?"

Louis shook his head. "You are a modern *Americaine*. A female leader. A role model for female students. And yet you kneel to me? Can you blame me for wondering why?"

Bishou gazed at him for a long moment. Then, quietly, she asked, "Is that what you see first when you look at me?"

Suddenly, Louis smiled. "Non. That is what I see on the second look. The first is a beautiful woman who miraculously loves me."

Bishou slid over and put her arms around his neck. "What I see is a man who miraculously allows me to love him." She kissed him.

After the kiss, he observed, "Carola used to kiss me to divert me from whatever question or doubt I had. You, Bishou—you use a kiss to seal the deal, don't you?"

Bishou chuckled. "I never really thought of it like that."

"I must get used to this—a kiss that means 'I promise,' not 'Don't pay attention to that other thing.' Because I still ask myself what is being sneaked by me." Louis sighed. "I cannot trust everything you do, and I am trying so hard. I am sorry."

"Louis, that's like a burn victim saying 'Please excuse my bandages,'" Bishou protested, stroking his neck and throat. "Of course you are cautious. If you were not cautious, I would wonder if you had any brains at all. Don't stop asking because you're afraid of hurting my feelings. Remember, I grew up with boys. My feelings don't get bruised easily."

"And I know you say less rather than more, when we are in company," he admitted.

"That's the academic world. It's small and gossipy. I think La Réunion is the same—and also, you were born here. You're family." She kissed him again. "You know how I look at the people around someone, and judge from their reactions. The people of La Réunion were happy to take you back, and they are proud of your business. Riding the buses, I have never heard one harsh word about you or Etien, even before anyone knew I came here to see you. That's a tremendous testimonial."

Louis had been smiling and stroking her back as she spoke to him. His anxiety faded. "There will be rough times," he warned.

"I don't doubt it for a moment. But these are not those times," she replied.

Chapter 9

They came back to find the house invaded by Howard boys. Bettina and Madeleine, giggling like schoolgirls, had fixed supper in the dining room for them. Bat stood up to hug his sister, and patted Louis's shoulder. "So! Lasted a day already. Can we move back?"

"Sure. How was the camping?" Louis asked the boys.

"A lot of fun. Mr. Campard came out and joined us, too. He taught us some songs in French," Gerry said.

Louis laughed. "He did?"

Bat smiled wryly. "Mme. Campard wisely stayed within doors."

"Did you all have a good time?"

"Yeah," said Bat, "we did."

"*Pardonnez-moi*, Madame Dessant," said Bettina, as she re-entered the dining room, "there is a telephone call for you."

Puzzled, Bishou asked, "Did they give a name, Bettina?"

"*Oui*." Bettina almost giggled. "Madame Howard."

Every Howard scrambled to the salon. Louis roared with laughter, and followed.

Bishou lifted the receiver from its resting place on the writing desk. "*Allo?*"

"Is that my little Bishou?"

"Yes, Maman, it's me."

"How is everything? Did the wedding go well?"

"It was great. Jean-Baptiste will have photographs to show you. And I will send back the lace—thank you."

"You don't need to send it back."

"Yes, I do. It was my 'something borrowed.' And Jean-Baptiste might need it for his own wife someday."

Bat, sitting nearby, snorted. Louis grinned.

"Well, perhaps. But I worry about him, you know? He should be married by now, or at least have a *petite amie*."

"He will, Maman, don't worry." Neither "twin" had found the strength to tell their parents about the helicopter pilot who died before she could return to the States to marry Bat. Only Bishou, Bat, and Louis knew that tragedy, the event that pressed Bat to urge his sister to marry the man she loved.

"So you were married—almost a day ago now, isn't it?"

"Yes, it's the afternoon of the day after our wedding."

"So you have had your wedding night. Are you happy?"

"Yes, Mama, I am."

"And is Louis happy?"

"I think so, yes."

"Jean-Baptiste didn't tell us much about Louis, you know. Only that he was the Louis Dessant of Dessant Cigarettes, and that you had met him at East Virginia University. And that he was a well-to-do widower. Was he very lonely?"

"Yes, Maman, I think so."

"And you love him enough to forget about teaching, and your degree?"

"Not exactly, Maman. I'm going to be an adjunct professor at the Université Français de l'Océan Indien, UFOI, the French university system out here. They are just starting an expansion, and things look really promising for the future."

"Ah, good! Unless—how does Louis feel about that?"

"Well—we've already attended one reception together. And we were both complimented on our good taste in choosing each other. So I presume things will go all right."

"That is good to know. May I speak to Louis?"

Bishou took the receiver from her ear, and regarded her husband. "Maman wants to speak to you."

Surprised, Louis took the phone, and sat at the desk. He was even neat and orderly in his telephone calls. "*Allo, Madame.*"

Then came the sort of conversation Bishou could imagine, only from hearing Louis's replies. Maman had apparently switched completely to French, and Louis answered accordingly.

"About myself? Well, I am an older man, thirty-six, and I run my own business.—No, I have a partner, my best friend, Etien Campard.—Yes, the Campards were our witnesses.—Jean-Baptiste? Non, Madame, he took Bishou to the altar.—Yes, father of the bride.—I was a widower.—No, I am not surprised Jean-Baptiste did not tell you that. It was ten years ago.—Yes, I was very young then. There are things I do not like to talk about, but Bishou knows." His voice gentled. "About you? I know that you are unable to walk very much.—Well, they have said nothing, but I am guessing you are very beautiful."

He smiled. "I have seen your children, Madame. In fact, I married one of them." This time, he laughed, obviously a laugh shared over the telephone. "*Non*, I don't know when we will get there, Madame. With my business, and other concerns, I do not travel much. In the summer, perhaps. I don't like snow.—Oh, yes, I went to school in France.—Non, in Lyons, not Paris. And I spent time in the Ardennes. That is where I learned to hate snow.—My mother died when I was seven. My father died fifteen years ago.—Yes, I do think of loneliness. I learned the tobacco business from him. I am proud of her, yes. And others compliment me on my beautiful, talented wife.—Children someday, I think.—Oh, yes, our house is big enough for them. Gerry and Andy have been great fun here. Jean-Baptiste took them, and the Campard boys, camping in the Campards' back yard." He laughed. "I imagine it was." He listened for a few moments. "*Oui*, I shall remember. *Au revoir.*" He handed the receiver back to Bishou.

"He sounds sweet," Maman said to Bishou.

"He is," Bishou confirmed.

"And he doesn't tell tales out of school, does he? 'There are things I do not like to talk about, but Bishou knows.' The question is—do you know?"

"Yes, Maman, I do."

"And you keep his secrets? Always remember to do that, Bishou. If your man wants to hide something away, let him hide it. If he's comfortable telling you his secrets, that's especially good."

"I know, Maman. You're right."

"Did you hear him tell me I must be beautiful?"

"Certainly I did, and he's right, you know."

"Oh, Bishou. You never change. Take care, *ma petite*, and put your brother on."

"Here's Jean-Baptiste. *Au revoir*, Maman."

Bat took the receiver from her, and began a syncopated conversation of his own. His laconic answers, so different from Louis's, highlighted his caution. "Yes, Maman, they did.—We spent a day together, had a good time.—Yeah, saw the Indian Ocean.—Pretty nice, what I can see.—No.—No.—Jet lag was worse for us than for her. She took the ferry partway, yeah.—Beautiful scenery. Volcanoes, ocean, blue sky. A lot like Hawaii.—Good seafood, too.—No, straight from the nets.—Couple more days. Then we'll head back.—Sure. Good-bye, Maman." He hung up the phone, and looked at his sister. "Think she's been in suspense, or what?"

"I'd say so." Bishou turned to Louis. "Sorry to dump that on you without warning."

Bat smiled at him. "Thanks for flirting with her a little."

"My pleasure," Louis replied. "She's rather nice, I think. Why did your father not get on the telephone?"

"He doesn't like it," Bishou answered.

At the same time, Bat made a face. "You might find this hard to believe, Louis, because Maman is in a wheelchair—but the only reason I could feel comfortable traveling with the boys was because I knew Maman was there to take care of Dad."

Louis looked surprised. "Not vice versa?"

"No," Bishou confirmed, "not vice versa. And yet—" She glanced uncomfortably at Bat, who gave her an imperceptible nod, "—Dad isn't exactly scatterbrained, either. They're not crazy. They don't need professional help."

"Yet sometimes you both talk as if they do," Louis said with an interested frown.

"Let me explain. When I was home this last time, Dad disappeared one day. He drove off in the car, no one knew where. Vanished."

"Mmph." Bat nodded. "I remember that day."

"He's a bad driver. He's been in many accidents. We panicked. I ended up calling the police chief—I'd gone to elementary school with him—to see if they could find the car on the road."

"We waited by the telephone for two hours, just sweating," said Bat.

"But at last we got a phone call from Dave Russell, the chief, saying the car was parked two towns away, and named the street. From there, Maman could guess. He went someplace he hadn't been for years. He'd gone to the Harvard Club. He's an alumnus of Harvard University."

"Did you fetch him back?" Louis wanted to know.

"Oh, no. Nor did we confront him, nor anything else that would start a fight. We just waited for him to drive himself home—which he shouldn't be doing, and yes, our nerves were on edge until he was safely back in the house—and I asked him how was his day. He said fine, he'd seen something in a newspaper somewhere he wanted me to have." Bishou smiled. "He'd brought me home the *Journal of Higher Education*, an old issue that was kicking around the Exeter Harvard Club. The article he'd seen was about UFOI. What did I think about teaching comparative literature in another country, Bishou? That was what Dad asked me. If Virginia, why not La Réunion? I will always wonder if he knew about you, or if he just thought it would be an exotic teaching post."

Bat nodded confirmation. "I wouldn't put it past him to leaf through my letters—and put them back so that I wouldn't notice. I wouldn't put it past his intuition, either. He has these *éclats*." Lightning-strikes.

"And that gave you the idea to come here?" Louis asked his wife.

Bishou blushed. "Well—it gave me an even better excuse to come here."

"And you credit him with insight," said Louis.

"It's hard not to. The day Bat and I took a walk, and had our long heart-to-heart talk about the future, down by the stream—when I came home, Dad just murmured to me, 'Have you and Bat got everything settled now?'" She shrugged. "So I just said yes. What else was there to say? He had known there was a problem all along, and knew just as well that we would deal with it."

"I begin to understand. It also makes me understand why neither of you has trouble with my memories of Carola. They are part of me, but they don't make me insane or evil."

"That's it," said Bat.

"And this woman, here," said Louis, pulling Bishou into his arms, "has learned how to deal with these men." He kissed her cheek. "She is one of a kind."

"I know, dammit," Bat grinned.

*

On Sunday morning, Bishou woke and nudged her husband. "Have you promised to go to Mass?"

Louis groaned. "*Oui*, I have promised."

"We had better start getting ready, then."

"*Embrace-moi, encore*," he murmured. Kiss me again. She wrapped her arms around his shoulders and kissed him lovingly.

"Mm. How difficult this penance is. I would much rather stay right here."

"I know you would. But we owe the Père."

"*Bien dit.*" Louis sat up, rubbed his eyes, felt his chin to see if he needed to shave. Of course he did; he always complained about having a "five o'clock shadow that appeared at three o'clock." Bishou washed up, and got out of the little bathroom so he could shave and get ready for church. She dressed, then stepped across the airy hallway to see if there was any activity from the guest bedroom.

She knocked when she heard voices. Andy opened the door, and peered out. "We're not dressed."

"You went to church on Friday. You don't have to go if you want to."

Andy grinned, a perfect image of Bat's naughty look. "It's no good. I already tried that one. Bat said up and at 'em. See you at church." Bishou laughed, leaned over, and gave him the same kiss she would have given Bat. Whatever that attitude was, it definitely ran in the Howard family.

Bishou turned as her own bedroom door clicked shut. She wore the print dress and little Sunday hat, and a pair of white heels, not nearly as elegant as her wedding shoes. She had managed to find white gloves at Mme. Ross's shop. Louis, also properly dressed for church in dark pants and brown jacket, raised an eyebrow. "*Prêt, cheri?*" Ready, darling?

"*Prêt, cherie.*"

Down the stairs, they went together, to the car. There was no sign of Bettina, but this was her half-day off; she would be back this afternoon. She might be at the church, anyway. Louis escorted Bishou to the little white car, and they drove off.

It was not much different from last Sunday, except for Bat, Andy, and Gerry crowding into the pew behind them. And, of course, Mass in French. Père Reynaud made eye contact with them during the procession, and at communion.

Standing outside after Mass, people came over to say hello to the Dessants, as if it were an ordinary event. *Well, from now on it will be*, Bishou thought.

Eliane and Marie, the sisters who owned Pension Étoile, came over and kissed them both. "Your wedding was beautiful! I cried the entire time. I wish you the best!" Marie said, while Eliane stood by. It was Eliane's hand Bishou clasped, knowing the romantic heart that beat beneath the stern breast. She felt the clasp returned, and saw Eliane's stiff lip tremble.

Mme. Nadine was also present. "I hope I can get you to come over sometime this week, with the dress," she said. "I have the illustrations, but I would like some photographs. It was an original design. The more records I have of it, the better. Tuesday, perhaps?" She glanced up at Bat. "Will you be busy, then, Monsieur Howard? A man in dark dress clothes makes good contrast in a photograph of a white dress."

"Not me," said Bat wryly. "The clothes would contrast, but the models would look too much alike."

"Then you, Monsieur Dessant?"

"I'm not photogenic."

"Photogenic doesn't matter when the man is famous. He is always photogenic," said Nadine.

"*Bien*, then, telephone us tomorrow and remind us," Louis agreed, to everyone's surprise. Nadine agreed, and moved off.

Bishou had caught Mama Jo's eye, or Mama Jo had caught hers. Mama Jo stood some distance away, in the yard, with her friends. Bishou motioned her over.

Mama Jo did not look uncomfortable as she and Armand merged with the white group still on the church patio. Bishou reached out a hand to her, and said to Louis, "*Mon mari*, this is Mama Jo, who did my hair for the wedding."

"Ah, how do you do, Madame," said Louis, as if this were a regular event.

"And Papa Armand, my personal chauffeur," said Bishou with a smile, and both men laughed.

"You drive the bus, Monsieur Armand?" asked Louis.

"Oui, Monsieur Dessant. We take good care of Madame Dessant, don't you worry."

"Or she will take good care of you," Louis returned.

"Just be careful for a day or two," Mama Jo said, "and watch out for your man, too." She touched Bishou's cheek, and left.

"What was that all about?" Bat asked, puzzled.

Louis explained, "Mama Jo's our local witch-woman, and she has taken a liking to Bishou. So, she watches out for her."

"You don't believe in all that?" Bat stared at his sister.

"No, I don't. But we had some good talks about many things while she worked on my hair, and she makes a lot of sense. Especially about men."

"I see," said Bat. "You talk woman talk."

"Do you want to come down to the factory?" Louis asked Bat. "I must get paperwork ready for a cigarette shipment to go out first thing tomorrow morning on the *Mauritius Pride*."

"Sure! The boys and I haven't seen the place yet." Bat deferred to his sister. "That all right with you? We'll take Louis to the factory and you can go on home?"

"Sure, that's fine with me," said Bishou. "I want to change out of my Sunday clothes and just relax."

"We won't be too long," said Louis, "because I want to relax, too. But I haven't been in the office since Thursday, and things have piled up."

"I'll bet they have," said Bat with a grin.

Louis gave Bishou the keys to the white car. "We will see you at the house." Then he kissed her, and joined the Howard boys in the gray Ford. She got in the white convertible, started it, and began the drive home.

Bishou was beginning to understand why people drove slowly

here. It was not only the grassy roads. There was also the smell of fruit, the call of birds, the flashes of colors in the trees, small animals leaping around... At last she turned on Rue Dessant, drove to the house, and parked the white Mercedes in front.

It was not yet noon, so Bettina and Madeleine weren't back yet. Bishou climbed the open stairs of the empty house to the third floor. She changed from her Sunday clothes into a housedress, and sat at the little desk with paper and pen, to write to Vig and Sukey Hansen, their good friends from the Tobacco Conference. She had yet to tell them what she'd done after visiting them in North Carolina.

The bedroom door was open. She heard the sound of the front door, got up, and moved to the hallway. "Is that you, Bettina?"

"Oui, Madame!" the voice called back. "Bettina and Madeleine. Do you want breakfast?"

"Yes, please! Louis and the boys have gone over to the factory. I don't know when they will be back. But I am very hungry!"

"We will fix a meal for you, and leave everything on the warmer for them."

"*Bonne idée*. I am writing a letter. I will come down in a while."

"Oui, Madame!"

Bishou smiled and sat down again. *Oui, Madame*. It really was like something out of an old movie.

"1 Rue Dessant, F-1001, Saint-Denis, Île de La Réunion. Dear Vig and Sukey," she wrote, "Don't worry, you won't need an interpreter to read this letter. On the other hand, you'll be glad to know that your predictions came true. Louis Dessant and I were married three days ago, in a little Catholic church here in Saint-Denis.

"I told you the truth when I said my business relations with East Virginia University prevented any personal relationships. But I admit I didn't tell you I planned to look him up after I got my degree, because you were right, Sukey, he was cute. And tell

Sondra I kept that number in my little black book—I knew good advice when I heard it.

"After I got my degree in hand, I flew from Logan Airport to Orly..."

Bishou looked up to see Bettina standing at the door, upset. "What's wrong?"

"Oh, please, Madame, you have a visitor."

"Who is it, Bettina?"

The housekeeper's face looked almost tragic as she brought in a calling card and handed it to Bishou. She read: ADRIENNE BOURJOIS.

Chapter 10

It took a moment to register. A calling card, a very Parisian affectation. Who was this? Bishou knew that Celie, the mail-order bride who was murdered on her way to La Reunion to marry Louis, was named Bourjois—and Bishou had now heard from several people about a vengeful sister who felt that Louis' seven years at hard labor had not been payment enough for his part in that crime. "*Adrienne Bourjois*. Oh, Lord." Bishou stood. Her face grew stern. "Thank you, Bettina, I will handle this. Where is she?"

"I showed her to the salon, Madame," said Bettina anxiously. "I didn't know what to do."

"You did right. Return to the kitchen. I may ring for coffee in a while, or not."

"*Oui, Madame.*"

Bishou climbed down the stairs, letting her heels clack, while Bettina stepped softly behind her. At the bottom, Bettina hurried to the kitchen while Bishou walked to the front room.

In a straight-backed chair sat a Parisian woman perhaps ten years older than Bishou, dressed in black. Her sharp-featured but nonetheless pretty face was directed at the entryway to the salon, and at Bishou. Her disapproval of everything about Bishou was palpable.

"Bonjour, Mademoiselle Bourjois," said Bishou, sitting in the chair near her. "What may I do for you?"

"Do for me!" she exclaimed angrily, pulling a newspaper clipping from her purse and flapping it at Bishou. "How can you contribute to such a disgrace?"

Bishou didn't need to see the clipping. She knew what it was, the announcement of their marriage in the Parisian newspaper.

There had been a larger article in the *Journal de l'Île*, more of a feature, rehashing the scandal of Louis's first marriage yet somehow kindly done. There had been a nice photograph in both. The *Paris Gazette*, loving its little bit of scandal, had picked up Louis's name for a wedding announcement—probably just to see what it would stir up. Well, here was what they stirred up.

"Are you such a fool that you don't know that you have married a murderer, or do you believe somehow that he is innocent of all the atrocities of which he was accused?"

"Neither. But I do believe he was as much a victim of Carola Alese as your poor sister."

The noise she made was one of disbelief and fury. "My sister Celie is dead because of him!"

"He did not murder your sister."

"He found out how she died—and he condoned it! He and I were supposed to share all costs in finding the criminal when she killed my sister and absconded with his money. He found her first, and killed our detective so he would not report to me! And then he took the murderess back, and treated her as his wife."

"And she finished ruining him," said Bishou steadily, "and left him for dead."

"And he forgave her and ran away with her again!" Mlle. Bourjois almost screamed.

"He was a fool," said Bishou. "You know he paid for that foolishness."

"He did not pay enough," Adrienne Bourjois said furiously. "Seven years, and they let him go! I testified against him. Again and again I wrote the Ministry of Justice, insisting that they make him pay for his crimes. And they released him! And now, *you* marry him, as if nothing ever happened!"

"Not true. Neither he nor I believe that."

"You are mad to marry him! He will find some way to kill you, you fool, and make it look like an accident! Don't tell me you love him. I have Celie's letters, where he speaks of love, and how many ideas they have in common. How he was looking forward to meeting her, what dress size did she wear and he would order the dress! Send a ring size, please! How he would meet her at the ferry, and he even had her photograph! Where did she end up? Over a ship's rail! What an accident! What makes you think *you* will be any different?"

"I can try to persuade you," said Bishou. "Will you have coffee with me?"

The true offended Parisian look. "Nothing in this house passes my lips. It would be poison."

Bishou sighed. "Mademoiselle Bourjois, I expected you to come here. I wanted to meet you. I hoped we could talk, and perhaps you could even find it in your heart to forgive Louis, just a little." At her snort, Bishou said, "Yes, I understand there is no forgiveness in your heart. I hoped there would be. But if you think there is no justice in the sentence Louis served in prison, at hard labor, and his status now, as a convicted felon, I don't know what would satisfy you. I will say, however, that God has been more merciful; Louis is completing his penance to be allowed back in the Catholic church." Bishou's voice gentled. "I understand that you and Celie were alone in the world—that this was an exciting, exotic adventure for her. It was for me, too; I understand what Celie must have felt. But I learned from her mistakes, I admit. I told no one where I was going, and I stayed away from low railings on the *Mauritius Pride*. But you were left alone."

"Don't patronize me," Adrienne Bourjois snarled. "You married him for his money, the same as the others."

"As a matter of fact, I did not," Bishou replied. "I am a teacher and I make my own living."

Mlle. Bourjois was saved the effort of replying to that statement by Bettina walking past the entryway to open the front door, and the sound of male voices. Bishou waited.

Andy and Gerry trooped in, kissed their sister, and sat on the couch. She could hear Bat dragging over a chair. She turned her head enough to see Louis from the corner of her eye. He walked into the room and took a good look at their guest. His knees gave out. He sank down on the nearest chair, white-faced, while Adrienne Bourjois glared at him.

They had come in boisterously, but Bat realized something was wrong. "*Bonjour*, Madame," he said to the guest. "We are sorry to interrupt your conversation." He glanced at Bishou interrogatively.

"Mademoiselle Bourjois, permit me to introduce my brother, Jean-Baptiste Howard," she said woodenly. "Bat, this is Adrienne Bourjois, the sister of the first Mme. Dessant."

"Carola's—?" Bat appeared puzzled.

"Non. Celie's sister. Practically speaking, please remember, I am the *third* Mme. Dessant."

"Ah," was all Bat said. However, he did an odd thing before he sat down—he dragged his chair into line between the visitor and Louis.

Louis, pale and silent, sat on a chair beside the doorway. Bat glanced at him, then at Mlle. Bourjois.

"You criminal!" she hissed at Louis. Louis remained silent.

"Please explain to me what happened," said Bat. Bishou recognized that tone—the tone of the Sergeant-Major with a new casualty washed ashore on his doorstep.

"My poor little sister, Celie, all excited with her correspondent, a man who worked for Dessant Cigarettes," Adrienne Bourjois hissed. Her eyes narrowed. "Trading letters back and forth, hers I still have—from that man! *That man*, who lied about his position, and did not tell Celie he was the owner of the business. *That man*, who learned that my poor sister had been murdered—and let the murder stand!"

"Hadn't I heard somewhere that he had been deceived and robbed, himself?" asked Bat, in the same neutral tone.

"He married the criminal—and then stayed faithful to her! Not to Celie, my sister! To the murderess and thief! He betrayed not only my sister, but me as well!" she raged. "I came here at his request—saw the photographs of the woman he married, saw it was not my sister. I saw Celie's unopened trunk—unopened because the criminal had no key for it, and would not dared to have opened it, anyway! Then he pretended to hire a detective with me, and killed the detective, so that he would not report to me!"

The calm look on Bat's face told Bishou that he had already discussed this with Louis. "What did you do then?" Bat asked.

"I notified the Sureté, through the Paris police," she said righteously. "It took the police another year to find them—but they did, in the Ardennes. And that vicious, evil woman got her just reward, a bullet in her head, fired by her own hand, so that she would not face the crime of murder!" Louis's gaze flashed up at those words, but he remained dumb.

"Why do you think Monsieur Dessant didn't do the same?" asked Bat reasonably.

"He's still alive, is he not? He has been given back his life and his money, has he not? Now he thinks he is free to live his life as if my little sister had not died for him!" The angry quaver in her voice was certainly genuine.

Suddenly, Andy interrupted. "Are we doing an intervention?"

Bishou stared at her adolescent brother. It had not even occurred to her. But she answered, even before Bat. "Yes, we are."

Adrienne Bourjois glared at her. "What is that?"

Bat slid easily into the conversation. "I am a soldier, Mademoiselle, a veteran of the American wars in Vietnam. Soldiers or their families often come to my house with problems. The problems may be alcoholism, drug addiction, mental illness, or an unforgiven sin. Very often, there is an angry confrontation. Like this one. So we try to talk it out, find a common ground, and make a new start."

"I don't want a new start!" she said angrily.

"Very likely," Bat agreed evenly. "But what I want is to keep you from shooting Louis Dessant with the gun you have in your purse."

Quicker than thought, she reached into her purse and pulled out a gun. Bishou was as paralyzed as everyone else in the room.

Mlle. Bourjois stood suddenly and shot.

Bat spun in his seat as the bullet rushed past his ear. A glass vase exploded beside Louis as he flopped forward in his chair to avoid the bullet.

Gerry Howard, all of eleven years old, grabbed her elbow. She fought him off. Another shot hit the ceiling.

Bishou was there in an instant. She wrestled the gun from Mlle. Bourjois's fingers, dropped it in the purse, and passed it to Gerry. He took off for somewhere, outside, like a linebacker heading for the goalposts.

"Do you think that's a good idea, before the children?" Bat asked mildly.

Louis spoke, in a hoarse voice. "For God's sake, Bat, if she is going to kill me, get out of the way. I don't want you hurt."

Just as evenly, Bat said, "Andy, keep Louis in his chair. Sit on his lap if you have to. You're heavy enough."

"Yes, sir," said Andy, standing in front of Louis, facing him.

The two housekeepers stood in the archway, terrified. "Monsieur!" Bettina wailed. "What is happening?"

"Non, it's under control," said Bishou. "Bettina, Madeleine, return to the kitchen, please."

"*Non, non,*" Madeleine protested. "If Monsieur Dessant is in danger, we stay here." The two women moved to either side of Andy, effectively barricading Louis from the rest of the room.

Bishou's voice was hard. "Don't you think that I could fold up Adrienne Bourjois into a little pile if I wanted to? But I don't want to. Now. Return to the kitchen, please. There will be no problem."

"Oui, Madame Dessant," said Bettina. They left reluctantly. Gerry reappeared in the doorway and came back to stand beside Mlle. Bourjois.

Gerry took her hand. "Please, madame. Sit down. I will stay here with you." Bishou pulled over a chair, for Gerry to sit beside her. Gerry did not release her hand.

The woman's gaze focused instead upon the boy beside her. Her anger faded. "You aren't afraid of me, are you?"

"Non, madame. I will stay here with you."

"Why?"

"Because Bat and Bishou both say that everyone needs a friend, no matter where they are. I will be yours."

"Just like that?" Adrienne Bourjois's voice quavered again. "Even though I almost killed your brother?"

"It didn't happen, did it? Bat's friends are all soldiers. They have all killed someone. You were just really angry."

She sat down, Gerry beside her, still holding her hand. Bishou also sat.

"Will you—" Bishou cleared her throat and tried again. "Would you care for some coffee, Madmoiselle Bourjois? If you truly think we are trying to poison you, Gerard will drink first from the cup, I promise."

"Even though I hate coffee," Gerry agreed.

Mlle. Bourjois's lips trembled as she looked down at him. It might have been a smile. She might have been ready to weep.

Louis staggered to his feet. Andy tried to help him to the couch, but Louis shook him off. Instead, he came to stand at Bishou's chair, within easy speaking distance of Adrienne Bourjois. In a tired voice, he told her, "You can see why I value them greater than gold. Adrienne, I am sorry. I can say so, now that the moment is past that you have tried to kill me. I didn't want to die—but if your bullet had hit me, I could have accepted my death." In alarm, Bishou rose from her chair as Louis sank down to the floor at Adrienne's knees. "I did wrong. I am sorry. Please forgive me. Please, Adrienne."

"That's a categorical apology," said Bat to her, neutrally. "Of course, if you really want to make him suffer, you can keep right on blaming him for everything that's gone wrong. Keep him begging for mercy, and deny forgiveness to him. Not very Christian, but perhaps it would make you feel better."

Adrienne's tears fell. She stroked Louis's hand, resting on the seat of her chair. "I'm a researcher, you know. We both were. Celie was so thrilled when she discovered you in *Business Biography*. She said, 'Now we will be happy. There will be money enough, and a husband, and children. You'll always have a place with us, Adrienne, and you can come and visit us at La Réunion. They say it's like paradise.'"

"Louis said that with Celie's death—not Carola's—he lost the dream. To marry, have a family, have a good life. It was all gone, turned to dust," said Bishou quietly. "He chased after Carola with a gun—very like you, Adrienne. And she told him, 'All right, shoot me, I don't care.' That was when he found out he couldn't shoot her."

Adrienne swallowed.

"I was in love with the girl I met in the letters," said Louis quietly. "Yes, we did have so many things in common. And when I met her—and she was so beautiful—she told me the photograph I had seen was a picture of her sister. She had been too afraid to send me one. Well, that was like the girl in the letters. I hadn't a clue. My friend Etien, too, a wiser man than I, he didn't catch on, either. He had seen her walking around Saint-Denis in places she ought not to be. She had kept him at arm's length, my best friend. He couldn't put it into words, but he tried to keep me from giving her joint rights to all my accounts, everything I gave her because I loved her and she was my wife."

"How did you first come to wonder if something was wrong?"

Bat prompted quietly. It was his "intervention" tone; Andy had been right.

Louis Dessant looked up from his spot at Adrienne's feet. "You mean, other than the wedding ring that didn't fit, and the trunk with no key? I got a registered letter at work," he replied with a smile.

Adrienne's tears fell thick and fast. "From me. Threatening him with a lawyer if he didn't tell me immediately that my sister was safe." She clasped his hand.

"I telephoned the house and told her to telephone you that she was all right. She said of course, and told me that evening that she had telephoned you and you were so relieved."

"And she lied, of course," said Bat. "Because she wasn't Celie. Celie was dead. She'd killed her and taken her place. Adrienne—forgive me for asking—but have you ever really grieved for Celie? I mean, is there a gravestone for her somewhere?"

"*Non.* She died in the Indian Ocean, between here and Mauritius. No body was ever found. My only sister. I have had nothing but my rage." She did not ask forgiveness, but she continued to stroke Louis's hand. "I suppose I should put a marker in our family plot, in Ivry."

"Don't you think the marker should be here, in the Dessant plot?" Bishou asked softly. "It would help to keep the tale alive. After all, she is the first Madame Dessant."

"I couldn't afford to come here to visit it," said Adrienne. "I sold everything I had to buy the ticket—and the gun."

"You didn't buy that gun," said Bat. "It looked like an old Mauser. Your dad's gun, maybe? Was he in the war?"

"My uncle's gun," Adrienne admitted.

"Well, you should decide where you want that marker," said Bat, "and plant it there. And grieve over it, too. You've never finished the job."

"No, I could not. Not with the trial, and Monsieur Dessant's imprisonment, and his prison hearings. I was there. I fought his release."

"You were living on your anger," said Bat. "Now you need to let it go."

"Stay here for a while, Adrienne," Bishou urged gently. "Stay. You say you have no sister. Nor do I. Why don't you stay until the boys leave for Orly, and all go back together, at least as far as Paris?"

Gerry brightened. "Yeah! You can show us the Eiffel Tower. I want to see it."

"I have climbed the Eiffel Tower several times," she said, looking down at him with a smile.

"You can tell him how to do it at dinner," said Bishou. "He wants to go sometime. You'll stay here, of course."

"Where's your luggage?" Bat asked, standing to get it.

"I have no luggage," Adrienne replied.

"Talk about passion," said Bishou. "You came here with a one-way ticket and a gun, didn't you?"

"Yes," Adrienne admitted, "I did."

"You really expected to be in jail tonight, for murder," said Bishou.

"I'm not giving the gun back," Gerry threatened.

"Don't. But she needs her purse, Gerry. And she needs a chance to clean the gun oil off everything inside," Bat contributed, adding, "I saw that it was dripping oil."

Gerry nodded, and left again for someplace.

"Well, crap!" said Bat, sitting down again. "Not so much as a nightgown and a toothbrush?"

"Oh, phooey," said Bishou. "We can dig up a toothbrush and hairbrush, and you can give her one of your pajama tops. There's room for two women in there."

"There is not," said Bat, grinning.

"Listen to him. And Adrienne will stay in the white bedroom."

Louis smiled weakly, and looked up from his spot on the floor. "That room has one disadvantage, Adrienne. There's a bullet hole in it." He pointed to the ceiling. Then he ducked as Adrienne Bourjois, weeping, very lightly boxed his ears.

Chapter 11

They ate dinner early in the day. Louis said grace, which they often did not do, and then let the conversation wander whither it would. Where it wandered, eventually, was to Paris.

"So were you scared, going up in that old rickety elevator, to the top of the Eiffel Tower?" Gerry asked Adrienne, wide-eyed.

"Oh, no. I had faith in it. It had taken many other passengers before me, surely. But it was odd, to feel it vibrating under one's feet." Adrienne regarded Bat. "Have you been there, Monsieur Howard?"

"Call me Jean-Baptiste," Bat said agreeably. "There are too many Howards here to distinguish them well. Oui, I went once, many years ago. I don't recall the ride. I just remember looking out at the City of Lights—that's what they call Paris, you know," he added to the boys. "It twinkled in every direction."

"Like stars." Bishou nodded.

"I have been there, and you make me feel as if I haven't," Louis told them. "My interests were restaurants, dancing, the cinema, and the news. You saw an entirely different side of Paris."

Bishou, sitting at the corner of the table beside him, smiled and said, "We'll go back some day and visit. You can see it with new eyes."

Louis smiled at his wife. "I would like that."

"I work for the Bibliothèque Nationale," said Adrienne, "as a researcher. Sometimes I work late, and walk home after work. Even from the ground, the lights appear magical." She smiled at Bat.

"Bishou and I have been there as tourists," Bat said. "It would be nice to go with a native, someone who really knows her way around. You might have us knocking on your door any day, pleading for a tour."

121

"That might be fun," said Adrienne with a smile. Bishou thought, *She's taken with Bat. I hope he's up to this.*

"You know," said Bat seriously, "I think it might be."

*

Louis changed into his pajama-bottoms while Bishou put on her lightest gown. They slid into bed as Louis shut off the light. The full moon shone in the window.

Louis sighed. *"Embrace-moi."*

"I am so happy to embrace you." Bishou wrapped her arms around him. "What a day. I am exhausted. I'm certain it must be nerves."

"Oui. Notice, please, I didn't faint. I was almost shot and killed, yes, but I did not embarrass myself by fainting. The only thing that could have been worse would be if Etien and Denise had showed up, snorting fire."

"I was afraid of that, too," Bishou confessed. "I'm surprised they didn't do something. If someone asks me tomorrow what the police were doing, stationed a mile from our house in surveillance mode, I won't be surprised."

"You think Etien might have called them? That would have been prudent, very like Etien." Louis sighed and pressed his face into her hair. "We were very fortunate."

"Most definitely. But if we introduce Adrienne as our sister-in-law, and treat her as a sister-in-law should be treated, I think she will be willing to accept it."

"I think so, too. Your brothers were wonderful, getting her talking about Paris. And you, telling about volunteering at the public library, and offering to take her on a tour of the university library. How did you know she was a consultant?"

"Twenty-one years as a researcher. That's a very active field right now. And she's in the French national library. I'll bet she's much in demand as a consultant, actually."

"Another career woman, like you."

"In a way, yes."

"I am going to have nightmares tonight. I hope you are prepared for it."

"I hope you won't, but I'm prepared, *mon cheri*."

"You and Bat made me think about things that hadn't occurred to me. Of course, once I married Celie, Adrienne expected to visit as my wife's sister, an honored guest. Of course she planned to go to parties, go shopping, visit the cafés—all those other happy things that are part of life on La Réunion, things that did not happen when her sister failed to arrive." Louis sighed. "Those two dull girls were going to have a romantic, happy life, and my money would help a bit, *oui*. Carola, though—she just wanted to take my money and get away from this dull life, to happiness elsewhere."

"It didn't work, did it?"

"It never could have worked, even if it had turned out the way it was supposed to." Louis nestled against her. "Carola gave all my money to her boyfriend—the man who actually killed Celie. Then he ditched her. That was how I saw her, accidentally, while I was recuperating from my first major nervous attack—she was a sales clerk at a department store, earning pennies because she was broke again. She had been suckered, too."

"What a circle of misery," Bishou murmured, stroking him.

"Mm, oui." Louis was silent for a moment. Then, in a different tone, he asked, "Bishou—what would you have done if she had killed me?"

"Killed you? *Mon amour*, I cannot even bear to think about that."

"Answer me, Bishou."

"There would have been two dead bodies for the coroner to scrape up."

"I gathered that, from the way you spoke to Bettina and

Madeleine. They certainly believed you at once." He kissed her cheek. "You are not really that vicious, are you?"

"About you, I am."

"Yes, I wondered." Louis kissed her cheek again. "Bat, he is the soldier. But he did not question you, either, *ma tigresse*."

"We have fought before."

"You and Bat? Ah. You do not mean with words."

"No, not with words. Football outside, soccer as they call it here, or American football, tag ball. But Andy and Gerry stay out of our way, and we mop up the field with each other until our anger wears off."

She felt him chuckle. "And who wins?"

"Bat ought to. But sometimes he concedes victory to me, if I'm angry enough."

"What makes you angry? I do not know."

"Bat lied to me about money, once. He said he was all right, when he was actually broke and had put all his money toward some friends in trouble, and finished himself off with my EVU payments. I got a black eye out of that, but I won. He got mad when I went to McGill University in Montreal for a degree interview, because he thought I was running away from problems in America—that was just after he joined the Marines. He sat on me until I agreed to scratch the Canadian universities off my list of possibilities."

Again, he chuckled. "And did you?"

"Not an issue. None of them offered me as attractive a deal as East Virginia University." Nor did she admit that she had kept looking in Canada, and she knew he knew it. "But Bat doesn't try to lie to me anymore, and I try to speak fairly about whatever the topic is on the table."

Louis stretched his arm across her chest, clasping her breast. "And what of us? We must not fight it out, need we?"

Bishou kissed his cheek. "Oh, *non*. All you need is to look at me with those puppy-dog eyes, and I will reconsider anything. You are my heart."

Louis rolled over, almost on top of her, and sighed, "*Ah, oui.*"

*

Bishou woke in the night, thinking she had heard a voice.

She had. It was Louis, next to her, talking in his sleep. He was trembling. "*Non, non.* Get out of the way!" Then, softly, he said a name. Not the name she was expecting to hear. "Bishou."

Softly, she murmured in his ear, "*Oui,* Louis, *je suis ici.*"

"*Si froid.*" So cold. Just what he had said when he collapsed in Virginia—except that he had called for Carola, then. It seemed a lifetime ago.

Bishou turned on the lamp, saw that Louis was still asleep, and dug another blanket out of the armoire. She wrapped it around him carefully, then turned off the light again.

"Bishou."

"*Oui,* Louis, *je suis ici.*"

He was still sound asleep, although his voice seemed pained. "*Je t'aime, je t'aime. Ma Bishou, non, non,* don't leave me."

"This *is* a nightmare," she murmured, wrapping her arms around him. "Non, *mon mari,* I am here."

He twitched, jumped, and suddenly sat up, gasping. Bishou sat up and turned on the lamp.

Louis looked at her, then at himself and the blanket wrapped around him. "My nerves," he said. "That is what makes me so cold."

"I thought so," she said quietly. "Here, roll over, let me rub some of Mama Jo's oil on your back."

"It will make me relax too much."

"Let us take that chance."

He set the blanket aside.

"And the pajama bottoms."

He slid them off, and lay face down. She rubbed oil on his back.

Bishou heard him sob, a small gasp. She reached in her drawer for a handkerchief and gave it to him. "It's just from relaxing, Louis. Let it out."

"*Non.* I don't like to weep in front of you."

"You won't," she said gently. "This is just part of the muscles relaxing."

"*Merde*, you can lie."

Bishou smiled and kept rubbing his back. "I love doing this to you. Your skin is so soft and warm."

"I thought I was the sensual one."

"You are," she told him, and Louis smiled and closed his eyes. It was a long time before she finished massaging him. She saw silent tears as he relaxed completely.

"You are not trying to arouse me tonight," he said.

"I want you to get a good night's sleep."

"I will be a wreck at work tomorrow. Good thing I got that cigarette shipment ready this morning."

"Mm, true."

"Bishou—what are we going to do about Adrienne Bourjois?"

"*Rien, mon treasor.* Have our meals with her, treat her like family, let her absorb our way of life, let her think. I think she'll come around."

"And Bat. Have you seen her look at him?"

"Well? I would rather she look at him than at you."

He sighed, reached over, and shut off the lamp. "I suppose that as long as she's not taking shots at me, I should be grateful."

"We'll be all right, Louis, watch and see."

Chapter 12

Breakfast in the morning was the first chance at Dessant normalcy, in a way. It was no longer a wedding day, Saturday, or a church day.

Bishou awoke at the sound of her little alarm clock. It was only six in the morning, but people here started early, while it was still cool. They took a two-hour break in the afternoon, when the heat was at its worst.

She could hear thuds and voices of the boys next door. The Howard boys were lively this morning.

Louis sighed and sat up. "At least I slept the night through," he said, rubbing his eyes and feeling his chin-whiskers. He staggered into the bathroom to wash up while Bishou changed clothes, and then they swapped places.

As he knotted his tie, he asked Bishou, "What did you plan for the day?"

"I think I'll need to take Adrienne into town for some cool clothes," Bishou replied. "Perhaps we could have lunch at Chez Ma Tante, or one of the other cafés."

"And the boys?"

"If they're making that much noise already, they're headed for the beach."

Louis laughed. "I was planning to take the car."

"No problem. Adrienne and I will ride the bus."

Louis opened his billfold, and gave her at least half of the bills in it. "Please plan to be home for lunch. In the afternoon, we must go to the bank."

"Oh. All right."

Louis glanced at her, but he was not surprised by her words or tone. "*Cherie*, you know we must. Also the lawyer, to change my will. However uncomfortable it makes you, I am nonetheless a wealthy businessman and must plan accordingly."

"I understand," Bishou answered. Then she asked tentatively, "You can get used to a wife who works, can't you?"

"Can I get used to being married to a beautiful college professor, you ask? Of course," he chuckled, bending over to kiss her cheek.

"That wasn't exactly what I meant. I meant, with a bank account of my own."

"Oh. We will discuss that at the bank, too."

"All right," she said uncomfortably, and left the room as he did.

Louis knocked on the opposite door. "Will you three be down for breakfast soon?" he called.

"All right, Louis, we'll be there," Bat's voice replied.

Bishou smiled and climbed down a flight, where she too tapped on a door. She heard, "*Qui est là?*"

"*C'est Bishou.* Please, Adrienne, come and join us for breakfast."

"*Deux minutes.*"

By the time they reached the table, Bettina was serving the meal. The *Journal de l'Île* by one plate indicated Louis's place. He seated his wife, let her pour his coffee, and sat reading while waiting for the others to join them.

In a few minutes, all the places were filled. Bettina hurried around the table, serving everyone, while they passed things to each other as well. Louis tossed his paper behind him, and joined in.

"How did you sleep, Adrienne?" Bishou asked her.

"Oh, soundly, *merci.*" She looked down at the drab clothes she wore for the second or third day. "I am afraid I need a change of clothes."

"I expected that. We'll go around to Mme. Ross's, and get you supplied. What about you, brothers?"

"*La plage,*" said Bat. Beach.

Louis smiled. "Bishou guessed that from the noise."

Bat grinned. "Yeah, one of those places rents surfboards. Andy wants to try it."

Adrienne's eyes widened. "Oh, *ma foie!* Like Hawaii?"

"*Oui*, like Hawaii."

"That could be dangerous."

"I wouldn't let them out there if they couldn't swim," Bat demurred, "but we'll probably have sore muscles tonight that we don't even realize we own."

"You will, I'm sure. I hope you have a good day," said Bishou.

Louis glanced at the clock, glanced at his wife, and stood. Bishou stood also, and accompanied him to the front door. She kissed him and nestled against him.

"Ah *non*, don't make it more difficult for me to leave than it is already," Louis murmured. "I will see you at lunch. *Au revoir, cherie.*" He kissed her again, slowly and gently. She stood in the doorway and watched him climb into the little car and drive off, waving goodbye.

The Howard boys trooped out, carrying towels. Bat kissed his sister. "See you sometime this afternoon. I think we're headed for Plage Est, but we'll see where we end up." The boys kissed her, too, and also left. If Bishou hadn't had a guest, she would have been tempted to go with them. But there was a guest.

Adrienne was pouring coffee at the dining table. She looked like another person now, different and peaceful. Her face didn't look hard, her blue eyes were calm, and her hair was rather pretty, brown with gold highlights. She smiled at Bishou, and refilled her cup, too.

"Merci." Bishou relaxed into the chair beside her. "I feel like we have just launched the first two assaults."

Adrienne actually laughed. "You don't need to entertain me, you know."

"But I want to, if you'll let me."

"I would like to see more of this island," Adrienne admitted.

"If you have errands to run, I wouldn't mind coming with you. Perhaps I could help."

Bishou looked up at Bettina, picking up things behind her. "Do you need anything from anywhere, Bettina?"

"No, merci, Madame. I telephoned the greengrocer and the butcher. They will bring things out later today. Do you know if you or Monsieur Dessant will be paying the bills?"

"Non, I don't know, not yet. That is one of the details I will work out with him later, who will pay the household bills. We haven't really had time to discuss it."

"Oui, Madame." Bettina left with her armload of soiled dishes.

Bishou fixed her coffee and drank thoughtfully.

Adrienne said, "This is your first working day as Madame Dessant, is it not?"

"Oui." Bishou focused again on her guest.

Adrienne smiled. "Whose first houseguest shows up the evening before with a loaded gun and a passion for revenge."

Bishou laughed, and felt the weight of the day lift from her shoulders. "Non, non, my crazy brothers were my first houseguests. How can you compete with them?"

Adrienne laughed sheepishly. "And—I confess—this coffee is rather good. I am sorry I passed it up yesterday, in my rage."

"If there is one thing I have learned, during the past year or two," said Bishou, "it is about passion. Both the good passion, and the bad." She patted Adrienne's hand. "Come. Let's go shopping."

"In La Réunion? Can it be done?"

"Sure, in both stores."

Now, Adrienne truly laughed. They finished their coffee, and Bishou went to the kitchen to tell Bettina and Madeleine where she was going.

The housekeepers were hard at work in the kitchen, and looked up as she entered. "Madame!" said Madeleine, sounding almost relieved.

"A mad weekend, yes?" Bishou asked with a smile.

"Oh, oui, madame," said Bettina fervently.

"Here are the plans, such as I know them," Bishou said. "Mademoiselle Bourjois and I are going shopping, to get her some lighter clothing for La Réunion—she is wearing winter Paris clothes. I am probably going to stop by the université, and we might stop at Chez Ma Tante. But I promised Monsieur Dessant I would meet him here when he came home for lunch."

"That is usually about one, Madame," said Bettina.

"Then Adrienne Bourjois and I will have just tea and biscuits at Chez Ma Tante, and leave room for a little lunch," said Bishou. "Monsieur and I have an appointment or two this afternoon, so Mlle. Bourjois might be the only one here, but she will be alone only briefly. My brothers will return from their beach day by then, I am certain. Dinner will be at the usual time, for all of us. And the boys might want a little supper later in the evening—you know what boys' appetites are like."

Madeleine was obviously relieved. "I did not know if you would understand what the mistress of the house needs to tell us, Mme. Dessant. And Monsieur Dessant told us nothing this morning, and left it to you."

"I will try to keep you apprised of what is happening in your own house," said Bishou with a wry smile. "And please ask me if you wonder if I have forgotten something. I may have."

"Mademoiselle Bourjois—will everything be all right now, with her?" asked Bettina anxiously.

"I think so," Bishou responded. "We'll go shopping, and do girls' things today. And—perhaps it is vulgar to say it—I think she is making friends with my brother Jean-Baptiste."

"I was wondering if you had noticed that, Madame," said Bettina. "He is making friends with her, too, you know."

"Well, he is a very attractive man," said Madeleine, "just like our Monsieur Dessant." Then she blushed.

"Oui," said Bishou gently, "and well I know it."

"We'll do our cleaning upstairs while you ladies are gone," Bettina resumed. "Then if either of you want a nap, or a bath, or to try on new clothes, everything will be ready."

"Excellent," said Bishou. "Then we will see you sometime after noon."

"Oui, Madame," they chorused.

Back in the dining room, Adrienne asked, "Is the household all set?"

"Yes. They'll clean the upstairs while we are gone, in case we need to rest from the heat when we get back. Oh, Adrienne, you definitely won't need that black sweater. Just leave it on a chair. Bettina can put it away."

"I am so used to Paris in cool weather," Adrienne explained.

"This is La Réunion in summer," said Bishou with a smile. "*Viens!*"

Adrienne almost had to run to keep up with Bishou as she strode down Rue Dessant. They waited for the bus. Armand slowed down while Adrienne hopped onto an outside seat. Bishou climbed on long enough to give Armand his money, then dropped into a seat beside Adrienne.

"Bonjour, Madame Bishou!" Armand greeted her cheerily. "Where are you going?"

"Rue Marché first," Bishou replied. "Armand, this is my sister-in-law, Mademoiselle Adrienne."

"*Bonjour*, Mademoiselle Adrienne!" the driver greeted her. "Welcome to our island. Did you come for the wedding? I don't remember seeing you."

"Non, I came later," Adrienne replied truthfully.

"Ah, well, you missed a good wedding. *Bienvenue!* Enjoy your time here, mademoiselle!" Armand laughed.

"*Merci*, I shall."

They watched mynahs and flycatchers, looked at cotton and tobacco and sugar cane in the fields, all those things Bishou had enjoyed on her first day on the island. At last, country gave way to town, and they were at Rue Marché, Market Street.

Adrienne changed into a sundress they bought at Mme. Ross's store. They bought underwear, and a second sundress. They bought a sunhat. Adrienne's own clothes went into the shopping bag. "Whew," said Adrienne. "I feel cleaner now."

"I imagine Bat's pajama top was clean, too," Bishou laughed. "Certainly not used by him. I don't know why he bothers to pack a set."

"It was still folded when he gave it to me," Adrienne admitted with a smile, "and he was not in the least embarrassed about it. Is he always like that?"

"Well, you know, Jean-Baptiste was a soldier, in charge of soldiers," Bishou replied. "A mother-hen for a battalion. His boys must wash up and look good, but that doesn't necessarily mean clothes that match. I don't think any man worries about that. Except, perhaps, businessmen like Louis. For them, it is their uniform."

Then they went to the shoe store. Bishou bought Adrienne a set of comfortable sandals, but also pointed out a daintier pair of white heels. "They'll go well with the sundresses when you dress up," Bishou said.

"Oh, this is too much to ask you to buy," Adrienne demurred, but it didn't sound as though her heart was in it.

"I think they'll look rather nice on you," said Bishou, and bought them.

They walked back a few blocks to Missy's bodega, which also sold sundries. Adrienne needed a hairbrush and toothbrush. Then, at Chez Ma Tante, they had tea and biscuits, as promised, at a café table on the sidewalk. They had just been served when Bishou heard a voice call, "Docteur Dessant!"

Bishou looked up to see Mme. Cantrell bearing down on them, with a male friend. "Bonjour, Madame!" Bishou greeted her. "How are you today?"

"Fine, thank you. We were just leaving, and I thought I would stop and say hello. Bertrand, this is Dr. Bishou Dessant, of the Humanities Department at UFOI. Bishou, Monsieur Bertrand Holian of the Bureau of Cultural Affairs."

"So nice to meet you." Bishou gave the gentleman her hand to shake. "Adrienne, this is Mme. Cantrell of the Library Society of Saint-Denis. Madame, my sister-in-law, Mademoiselle Adrienne Bourjois." Exactly the kind of social life Louis realized the Bourjois girls had expected on the island.

"How nice!" said Mme. Cantrell. "I hadn't realized your brother was married."

"*Non*, he is not," said Bishou. "It is my husband who was married. He was a widower when I married him."

"Oh," said Mme. Cantrell apologetically to Adrienne, "I forgot. How I put my foot in things. Forgive me."

"Certainly," said Adrienne.

"And how are you finding married life, Bishou?" Mme. Cantrell boomed. "Already a little dull, eh?"

Adrienne smiled as broadly as Bishou, aware of her own part in dispelling the dullness. "Not really," Bishou replied.

"Monsieur Holian is always looking for new blood for the Cultural Commission." Mme. Cantrell beamed at them. "You should both consider giving him your time."

"Ah, non, Monsieur, not yet," Bishou replied. "I am still finding my way through a fresh job and a new marriage. And my sister-in-law will be returning to Paris."

"Paris! Oh, my goodness. I hadn't realized the Dessants still had relatives in Paris."

"Not exactly," Adrienne replied. "I have a job there. I am a senior researcher at the Bibliothèque Nationale."

"Oh, my goodness!" said Mme. Cantrell again. Her companion's eyes widened.

"Well!" he exclaimed. "Mme. Cantrell has been telling me of

the talent that abounds in the Dessant family, and I thought she might be exaggerating. But I see she was not!"

"Have you been there for long?" asked Mme. Cantrell tactlessly.

"Oui, for twenty-one years."

"*Ma foie!*" Madame exclaimed, "one would never suspect it from looking at you."

"You are kind, Madame."

They made their excuses and their goodbyes, and went on their way. Both Bishou and Adrienne waited until they were well out of sight before they burst into laughter.

"Well!" said Adrienne, "some types are universal, aren't they?"

"All the subtlety of a volcano. But, I understand, a good heart."

Adrienne made a face, and drank tea. "The université might force you to be on a local commission, as a representative of the department, if they think it would be a good move politically, Bishou. I've seen that done before. It might be a good idea to put yourself on some local or academic board you like, before they issue any ultimatum."

"I will keep your advice in mind."

Adrienne sighed. "Me, giving you good advice. And only yesterday I was making a mad fool of myself."

Bishou put her elbow on the table and rested her head on her hand with a smile. "Adrienne, you are speaking to someone who has spent far too long in the field of literature, studying passion. Your passionate love, and equally passionate rage, are the marks of a good woman. Don't apologize any more, no more than Louis should."

"He was quite abject in his apology."

"He has been thoroughly raped," said Bishou, "as thoroughly as any virgin. Even now, he is hurt and bewildered by everything that happened to him. Little by little he begins to understand, and recover."

"I imagine prison didn't help," said Adrienne thoughtfully.

"No—but nothing would have, at that time. He was beyond help then. And now, he has paid the State for his crimes, and he is paying the church for all the commandments he has broken."

"I saw that he wears a penitent's cord beneath his day-clothes."

"Is that what one calls it? Yes, he does. I was so afraid Père Reynaud would just charge a fee for an indulgence—I am so glad he is making Louis work for his penance, and think about things."

"But, penitence notwithstanding, you and Louis—you are lovers, are you not?"

"Certainly we are."

"Do you plan to have children?"

"Yes. I would like a little Celie-Ange, myself." Celie-Angel.

"Do you think you might already be pregnant?"

"I might be. I don't know. It is a natural part of life, and I have no intention of thwarting Nature."

"That is good to hear. I had so hoped to become an aunt—" Adrienne bit her lip.

"You may still be," said Bishou.

Adrienne placed her hand on Bishou's. "Then—when you are ready to christen Celie-Ange—telephone me."

"You have my promise."

"You and Jean-Baptiste, and your brothers—you are rather independent of your parents, are you not?"

"Yes and no. Our mother is in a wheelchair. Our father forgets things. Jean-Baptiste and I made it our business, long ago, to be certain that Andre and Gerard did not lack for anything because of that. We determined until Gerard is eighteen, one or other of us would always be at home with our parents and with the boys. It—" she paused, but could not find a simple way to say it, "—it has proved necessary."

"But you got your doctorate. Jean-Baptiste served in the military."

"We took turns. It was part of our deal with each other."

"Ah, I see." Adrienne was very thoughtful. "Forgive me for sounding rude, but—are you just transferring your mothering instincts to Louis Dessant?"

"That's a legitimate question. I wondered, a little bit, myself. But I think the answer is no. I hope we have children, yes. If we do, I hope I will know what to do for them. But Louis himself? Non. He is a man—an incredibly attractive, sexually mature man. We are a man and a woman together, husband and wife. There is no mothering there."

"And you and Jean-Baptiste?"

"*Nous sommes les jumeaux.* The twins together, mock parents together, brother and sister when apart." Bishou drank her tea, and smiled. "We can balance a checkbook, change the oil filter on the car, call in a plumber, or take everyone to the cinema."

"Family survival skills," said Adrienne with a wry smile. "As I once did for my little sister Celie."

"That's it, exactly. Survival skills. That is what Jean-Baptiste and I do together, survive. But there is much more to life than merely survival." Bishou did not feel comfortable telling her about Amy. Let Bat tell his story, if he wished. Not her.

Adrienne was lost in a memory. "We were alone in the world, after Maman and Papa died—Maman of cancer, and Papa of a heart attack, within a year of each other. I so felt the responsibility for taking care of my little sister. And she was so—so starry-eyed, Bishou. Everything would be wonderful. She would place marriage advertisements, and Prince Charming would appear and carry her off, and we would all be happy forever after. And then my baby vanished, and I just went mad."

"Well, you have met Gerard—my little brother, Gerry. I am just as certain that Jean-Baptiste and I would go mad if anything happened to him."

"But you let him take my gun and run off with it."

"The Howards are a team, not a parental unit. Gerry and Andy are both part of that team. We never replace our parents, just supplement them."

"Hm," said Adrienne. "You decided that long ago, did you not?"

"Yes, when our father's memory first started to disappear. We felt that our brothers had a right to the life of normal boys, and it would be the duty of Jean-Baptiste and me to make sure they had that opportunity. Above all, they needed security and trust."

They finished their tea, and hunted up the bus stop. Soon, another island bus came by, driven by a different Creole driver. Bishou laughed, climbed inside, and dropped four or five Dessants in his hand. "So how are you related to Papa Armand?"

"Son-in-law," the driver replied promptly, grinning. "Merci, Madame Bishou. Bonjour, Mademoiselle. Where to, *université?*"

"*Oui, université.*"

Sitting beside Bishou in a cramped, crowded bus, but smiling, Adrienne asked, "Are they all related?"

"Even my hairdresser," Bishou confirmed with a smile.

"I thought your hair looked rather nice. Rather—free and natural," Adrienne said. "If I was going to be here longer, I would hunt up your hairdresser, but not for this short a trip."

"Next time," said Bishou, and Adrienne chuckled.

They got off the bus at the Université stop. The gates and courtyard of UFOI, so tiny and provincial and quaint, amused Adrienne, compared to what she knew in Paris. She walked with Bishou to the Humanities building, and entered the front office with her.

Mme. Ellis stood up immediately. "Dr. Dessant! Your timing couldn't be better. I just finished typing up your contract!" She brought it to the front counter.

Bishou read carefully. Sure enough, it was a one-year teaching contract for an adjunct part-time professor of comparative literature. She passed each page over to Adrienne as she finished reading it.

"This is good," Adrienne murmured. "You have medical rights

to the university hospital. I hadn't realized there was a medical school attached to this. The medical and pension benefits are pretty consistent with my own."

"And where do you work, Madame?" asked Mme. Ellis.

"Bibliotheque Nationale," Adrienne replied.

"What!" Mme. Ellis exclaimed.

Bishou looked up from her paperwork. "Oh, *mes apologies*, Mme. Ellis. Adrienne, Mme. Ellis of the Humanities Department. Madame, Mlle. Adrienne Bourjois, my sister-in-law." They greeted each other.

"What do you think?" Bishou asked Adrienne of the contract.

"It's all right. Are you satisfied with the wage?" Adrienne returned.

"It's a wage appropriate for a doctorate, and they've spelled out my class-hour obligations fairly well. I don't think I'll really know until I try it for a year."

"And vice versa," said Adrienne. "You may find that your other obligations eat up too much of your time."

"I was about to mail this to you, certified mail," said Mme. Ellis. "Why don't you take it with you, to study, and just give me a receipt?"

Bishou nodded, wrote on a piece of blank paper that she had both copies of her contract and its contract number, and tucked the contract and its copy into her purse.

"By the way, Dr. Dessant," said Mme. Ellis, almost blushing, "I truly enjoyed your lecture."

"Me too," said one of the other, younger, secretaries.

Bishou thanked them, and they left the office. They went back to the bus stop, and took the next bus for Rue Dessant. As they rode, Bishou told Adrienne about the expository lecture she had given. It was a pleasant ride back into the countryside. At last, their stop arrived. They hopped off the bus and walked up Rue Dessant.

Chapter 13

The white car and the yellow Panhard were parked in front. It was well past one o'clock. Louis and Etien were at table. The men stood as the women entered the dining room. Adrienne was introduced to Louis's shy, bespectacled business partner. Bishou and Adrienne took their packages upstairs, washed up, met again outside Adrienne's door, and came down to luncheon.

Louis explained that Etien would be needed at this afternoon's business appointments, so he had invited him home for lunch. Bishou could see, however, that Etien had been on pins and needles about Adrienne. He needed to see for himself that everything was all right. As Bishou and Adrienne talked about their morning shopping trip, tea break, and trip to the université, Etien relaxed visibly.

At last, they excused themselves to Adrienne, who announced she had no plans but a nice bath, a try-on of the new clothes, and perhaps some laundry, and went back out to their respective automobiles.

Louis and Etien pulled up in front of Caisse de La Réunion, the Bank of La Réunion, at the same time. Louis and Bishou waited at the door for Etien and they entered together.

Louis walked to the receptionist and said, "Dessant? We have an appointment with Monsieur Mouillard."

"Ah, *oui*, Monsieur Dessant. *Un moment, s'il vous plaît.*" The receptionist pushed a button on her telephone. "Monsieur Mouillard? Monsieur et Madame Dessant and Monsieur Campard are here."

They waited only a moment before a respectable graying banker appeared, making a beeline for Louis. "Ah, Monsieur Dessant," he said, reaching out a hand. "So nice to see you again."

"*Bonjour*, M. Mouillard," Louis greeted him. "*Ma femme*, Bishou—"

"Mme. Dessant," the banker greeted her, clasping her hand.

"—and of course, Monsieur Campard you know."

"Certainly. Welcome, welcome. Please, come into my office."

Bishou was aware of almost a pre-concerted effort as she walked between the men, into the banker's private office. Louis and Etien knew where to sit without the banker motioning to seats. There was no question that Etien was tense. *They've done this before*, she thought suddenly. *They're repeating exactly what they did with the first Mme. Dessant.*

Bishou met the banker's gaze. He was staring at her. She raised one brow. M. Mouillard saw, dropped his gaze, and tried not to smile. He'd been tense, too.

Louis was unheeding. "Monsieur, we must arrange my wife's signatures on my accounts."

M. Mouillard stared. "All of them, Monsieur?"

"Oui, all of them."

Bishou and Etien, both equally surprised, spoke at once. Etien halted, and motioned to Bishou to speak.

"Louis, I am not sure that is such a good idea. I was thinking more of a household account, where both you and I could transfer funds to pay household bills—"

"Yes, that would be a good arrangement." Etien almost interrupted her in his anxiety.

Louis Dessant's hand hit the arm of his chair imperatively. "*Non*." At their silence, he said determinedly, "Above all, I *must* be able to trust again. I *must* be able to trust my wife, do you see? I *must*."

Etien Campard sighed, knowing he had just hit bedrock.

Bishou sat back in silence, meeting her husband's gaze. At last, she said quietly, "I see you have thought about this."

"Assuredly," said Louis. "It isn't about the money. It is about the trust."

"Monsieur Mouillet's job," Etien interjected mildly, "is about the money." At least he had learned not to take Louis head-on. "How best to satisfy him? And, for that matter, me? We're in the same room, in the same chairs, you know."

Louis smiled, across Bishou, at Etien. "At least this time, you are admitting you're frightened, *mon frère.*"

"Petrified," Etien admitted.

His admission made them all laugh, including M. Mouillet. The banker said, "For all the conversations in this office about love, trust, and money, my job never gets any easier. The final decisions, of course, are yours, Monsieur Dessant. But I encourage you to work this out among you. Monsieur Campard is your partner in business. Mme. Dessant is your partner in life." *That was the perfect thing to say,* Bishou thought.

"Louis, I am going to be receiving a université paycheck," Bishou said. "It has been my intention all along to open a small account here, and use that paycheck as my *argent.* I don't want to take and take and take from you. I don't want to be a parasite— and you don't like parasites, either." Despite herself, her voice gentled. "I did not marry you for your money."

Louis smiled at her. "I know. We can discuss why you married me later. But I want to *give* you things. That's different from a woman who takes everything from me, ma Bishou."

M. Mouillet said reasonably, "Might I suggest a savings account for you, then, Mme. Dessant? As a separate account, it carries separate government insurance, and if you won't be writing checks on it—just cashing paychecks or depositing to your savings—it might be all you need."

Bishou turned to Louis and smiled. "And it falls under government guidelines for full reimbursement if the bank fails— unlike your accounts, Louis, which have too much money in them to qualify. So if we must move to a little apartment in Saint-Denis if our bank's fortunes reverse, we will not starve."

Louis eyed her for a moment. "How do you know so much about government bank insurance?"

"Are you kidding? I'm from Boston. The motto of the entire city of Boston is 'Don't touch the principal.'"

Monsieur Mouillet snickered appreciatively at a banking joke, which he was sure to be sharing with his friends at dinner tonight. "Madame, do you have any familiarity with bookkeeping? Truly, if you can journal what you spent on which purpose, the drawing account will not matter. The journaling would also help for tax purposes, not to mention such things as entries for a clothing allowance, or a grocery allowance." He was using financial terms with someone he knew would understand them.

"Who reconciles your bank accounts?" Bishou asked Louis.

"Anna and Claire," both men replied at once.

"Good. They double-check each other, and have the business's interests at heart," said Bishou.

Etien admitted, "That was one of the changes I made—after— after our last major mistake."

"It was a sensible thing we should have been doing all along," Louis agreed, "but it took a disaster to see it."

"They are good women, too," said Bishou.

"Oui, they are," said Etien.

"You must have been responsible for a great deal of reinforcing of the business," Bishou said to Etien admiringly. He blushed as if he had been told he was a candidate for Mister Universe.

Louis chuckled again. "We will buy each other drinks later," he said. "Now, let's settle this."

"*Bien, mon mari.*" Bishou sat forward, paying attention to him. "Tell me what you want."

"Now those are the words I like to hear from my wife," said Louis, and Etien grinned.

"Do you think we should have two checking accounts, though?" she asked, "just to make certain they're insured? One for daily use and one for special occasion?"

The banker jumped in. "The special-occasion one, if only two or three checks are drawn on it per year, can earn a higher rate of interest. There is no interest on an ordinary drawing account."

Louis usually made snap decisions, and this was no different. He looked calculatingly at Bishou, then at Mouillard, and said, "*Bon.* Split my personal drawing account down the middle, Monsieur Mouillard, half in a regular drawing account and half at the special rate. The business account, monitored by Mlle. Aucoeur, which now has my name, Etien's name, and the company treasurer's signatures authorized for it, you will also add Mme. Dessant's name, and we will change the rules on that account so that any check drawn for over one hundred thousand francs must have two signatures. *D'accord?*"

M. Mouillard nodded, taking notes. "An excellent idea."

Etien leaned back, looking relieved. "I like that, too."

"My personal accounts, though." He looked at Bishou. "Joint. Either signature for any amount."

Bishou took a deep breath, and dropped her gaze. "As you wish, *mon mari.*"

"And a separate little savings account of your own. To make you feel better. A passbook account."

M. Mouillard excused himself for a moment, to get the paperwork going on these new accounts and changes. While he was gone, Louis moved his chair so that he was nearer Bishou.

Louis kissed her hair and murmured, "I know you don't like handling other people's money, ma Bishou, but you have done it for your parents. You and Bat have paid their bills capably. And, you and your brother have taken care of your parents' income taxes for countless years. This is no different."

Bishou could have given several different replies. Instead, she reached up to his face, and kissed him gently. For a moment, he looked surprised. Then he smiled. There was a light in those brown eyes that she could never have imagined.

Monsieur Mouillard breezed back in, with forms for them to sign. There were even forms for Etien, to authorize changes on existing accounts, as well as forms for new accounts, closed accounts, special accounts. The business was concluded at dizzying speed. Bishou found herself tucking a savings passbook in her purse, already containing an opening deposit of a hundred thousand francs, from which she'd had to talk her husband down from five hundred thousand. There had also been authorization forms for the printer to print new checkbooks for all the drawing accounts, since there was no account except the basic checkbook that remained unchanged.

Once outside the bank, Etien said, "Whew." Privately, Bishou agreed.

"Now the lawyer," said Louis, looking down the block at another building in the distance.

"You don't need me for that." Etien leaned over and kissed Bishou. "Will Denise and I see you both for dinner on Friday?"

"Oui," said Louis. "Make plans for us, *mon ami*. We will be there."

"See you at work tomorrow," said Etien, getting back in the Panhard and driving off.

They walked down the street to a plain-looking stucco building, with a solicitor's shingle hung out. These people were ready for Monsieur Dessant. In a few minutes, he and Bishou were in the lawyer's private office, while they consulted about spousal benefits, the disposition of the business, and heirs. The lawyer promised to have the document ready for Louis's signature in two days, and in the meantime, the old will would remain in effect, he warned. No mention of a wife and the property equally divided between the Campard children. The lawyer himself was the executor of the estate—him or his law office. Bishou was rather glad of that; she was afraid Louis would nominate Bat as executor, which might be sticky, as he was an American.

Louis chuckled as he helped her into the car. "You look numb."

"I feel numb. Louis, a new professor makes 1200 francs per week, maybe."

"Really? I judge prices by what a pack of Dessants costs." He was unperturbed as he got in the driver's seat and began the drive out of town.

She placed her hand on his arm. "Louis, I'm drowning in money."

Louis laughed. "You little college student, watching every franc. Forget the money, *ma Bishou*. Just forget about it. That business is over. You know better, don't you? Life is worth much more than money."

"'The love of money is the root of all evil,'" she quoted.

He nodded. "The love of it. Not the money itself. It is there to buy food and shelter. No one likes to be robbed, myself included, but that is because it is a mark of disrespect, not because it is a red column in the ledger."

"I know. You are making perfect sense," she admitted.

He glanced at her as he drove. "And," he added, "if I ever say anything different, just start unbuttoning your blouse. I will forget my entire argument instantly."

"What's inside my blouse is not that valuable."

"To me it is."

Chapter 14

Bettina opened the front door as they approached. They saw a light in the salon, and glanced in. Surprisingly, Bat was sitting in Louis's usual place on the couch, with his lamp. Even more surprisingly, Adrienne was curled up next to him, barefoot, looking at something in his hands. "Bonjour," Bat greeted them. "The boys are at Campards'. Want to see how pretty you look?"

"Are those the wedding photographs?" Louis asked. He waved Bat back to his seat when he started to move. "*Non, non, mon frère*, stay where you are." He turned on another lamp, drew over a chair, and examined the photographs as Adrienne passed them to him. Bishou looked over his shoulder. *Thank goodness*, she thought, *not like those stilted French photographs*. Here were the Dessants, the Campards, and the Howards, smiling at each other. Here was the wedding breakfast, in the yard. Here was one with the Prefect and his wife in casual clothes, sharing a joke with them. And one of Bat pouring champagne for the American ambassador and his wife.

"We don't look like corpses propped up, do we?" said Bat.

"I was thinking the same thing," Bishou agreed.

"Pfui." Adrienne slapped Bat's arm disapprovingly, and shook her head. "You are all beautiful. Here's the one that was sent to the *Journal de l'Île* and the *Paris Gazette*." Louis and Bishou, smiling slightly at each other. "Are you putting together a wedding album?"

"I am," said Louis, at the same moment Bishou said, "He is." Then Bishou added, "Louis is far more organized than me about such things."

"Pfah," said Louis. "This from the woman who just finished a doctoral dissertation." The pair on the couch was laughing at them. *They really mesh well,* Bishou thought suddenly. *How did I miss this?*

"How did you spend your afternoon?" Adrienne asked them.

Louis shook his head. "Signing papers. Bank accounts. Wills and letters of intent."

"Lotta responsibility," said Bat in laconic English.

Bishou nodded. "Burned out and crashed. Needed to come up for air."

Adrienne looked blank. Amused, Louis translated into French for her. Adrienne smiled understandingly. "Money is like water, isn't it? One misses it if it's not there, either to bathe in or to drink. But otherwise, nice people don't think twice about it."

Louis laughed. "That is a better explanation than mine, *ma soeur!*"

"How did you spend *your* afternoon?" Bishou asked them.

"Oh," said Adrienne, "I went upstairs and took a bath, then changed into these new, pretty clothes. Then I asked Bettina to do some laundry for me, and she said she was happy to. By then, Jean-Baptiste was back. He had stopped at the wedding photographer, and picked up the photographs. So we have looked at them."

"How much do we owe you?" Bishou asked him.

Bat named a figure. "Since we'll be going home soon, I won't say no to some money for them."

"I'll give it to you tomorrow morning. I don't think I have that much cash in the house," said Louis.

"All right. Cash makes no enemies."

"Will it bother you to receive it in francs?"

"Not at all. I'll have a use for it, sooner or later."

"And I think we've already put Caisse de La Réunion to the test enough," Bishou said to Louis. He smiled agreement.

Bat looked down at Adrienne, leaning against his arm. "Want to go over to the Campards with me? I think these two want to be alone."

"*Bonne idée,*" Adrienne agreed. "Let me get my purse."

"What for?" Bat asked. "So you can have your identity card on you if I drive off without you?"

"Don't be foolish, and let me get my purse," Adrienne shot back, leaving the room.

"That's telling him, Adrienne," Bishou said approvingly, in a low voice.

"Supper at seven," said Louis. "It will be cooler by then."

Bat rose from the couch. "All right." He smiled, that cynical smile, and went out the front door. They heard the rasp of a match as he lit a cigarette on the way. Then they heard Adrienne's little footsteps, coming down the stairs.

"Enjoy yourselves," Bishou called.

"*Aussi,*" Adrienne laughed. They heard the door close behind her, then heard her voice and Bat's.

Louis shook his head. "Mon Dieu, there was my greatest danger, going away happily, with friends."

"I know." Bishou stood, and reached out her hand to Louis.

Louis smiled. They climbed the stairs to the third floor together.

Louis closed the bedroom door behind them, turned, and took off his shirt. He laid it on the bedroom chair. His other clothes soon followed.

Bishou washed her makeup off. She came out to a naked man, who embraced her and pulled her clothes down from her shoulders. In a few moments, she was naked too, and they were lying upon the bed together.

"Paradise," they said at the same time.

Bishou pressed her chest against his, and kissed his face. "I never thought I would be doing this with a man of my own."

"I had lost all hope of ever doing this again." Louis stroked her. Resting comfortably against her body, he kissed her breasts and said, "These end arguments, you know."

"I don't know. I give you whatever you want, *mon mari.*" She gasped as his lips and teeth touched her breasts, and his fingers stroked and probed. This mad feeling—this was what desire was all about. "Ah, *oui, oui.*"

She felt Louis chuckle. "This is what you want, *ma femme?*"

"Oui, Papa."

"Why Papa?" He slid up more solidly on her body, and added, "Never mind."

Bishou let him stroke her breasts. Apparently they fascinated him. Louis lay on one side, tracing a path with one finger. They lay comfortably like this for a very long time, watching the sun set, hearing the evening noises of the birds outside.

"Here," Louis said at last, in that peaceful, contented voice, "your body is like the Goddess, in the old stories, la Mère de la Réunion." He tweaked one nipple, then the other. "The mounds of the volcanoes. Piton de la Fournaise, Piton des Neiges." His finger traced a line to her navel. She took in a breath as he pushed his finger in her navel. "A caldera, une Cirque." His finger drew a line down far beyond her navel. This time, when he pressed with his finger, she cried out. "Another caldera, une Cirque."

She fought to control her breath. "Doesn't that legend say— that Father Sky comes to rest on Mother Earth? Isn't that what they say when the clouds rest on the island?"

"Oui, it is." He smiled, and rested himself on top of her body. He kissed her lips again and again. Bishou loved his soft lips. She wrapped her arms around him and stroked him while she returned his kisses. Of course, she really had no standard of comparison; but she found it hard to believe that other lovers made love this strongly, this often. Maybe Mama Jo had guessed what Louis's experiences had done to him, or guessed how a body like Bishou's would excite him.

After this round of lovemaking, Louis took her in his arms and murmured, "I think I heard the boys come back. We must get up and dress for dinner."

They went downstairs to find the boys and Adrienne already at table, having lemonade and waiting for them. Now Bettina and Madeleine served dinner. It was a cheerful, happy family dinner—so unlike what Louis was used to!—that made them laugh and laugh.

Bishou had called him Papa. Surely Louis had to realize that, soon, the laughter would come from their own children around this table.

*

A bird chirped outside the bedroom window and Bishou woke. Beside her, Louis slept soundly. The sun was starting to rise. Bishou slid out of bed, slipped on her robe, and crossed barefoot to the bedroom door. She opened it quietly.

She heard a gentle creak on the stairs. There was enough daylight now for her to see the figure creeping quietly up. She stepped into the hallway, slipped the shoes out of his hand, and set them outside the door of the guest bedroom.

Bat's eyes were as good as hers. She had not surprised him. He let himself be drawn over to the airy, open stairwell, and stepped out onto the landing with his sister.

"Were you laying for me?" he asked in a very low tone.

"Not really. The birds woke me up."

"Me too. I told her I'd better go back upstairs, or the boys would miss me." He paused, leaning against the railings. "You shocked?"

"Truthfully? No. You've always liked little women, brother."

Even in this light, she saw his smile. "Yeah, she's tough, but she's still a dainty little *Parisienne*."

"She's had to fight her way in the world, just as we have."

"Mmph." It was a gentle sound of agreement. "She just took my hand and pulled me into her bedroom, and I didn't exactly say no."

"I never thought you were celibate, brother."

"At home, I am." Bat felt in his pockets, found a cigarette, and lit it. "The day you spent with her made all the difference, you know. She said she feels normal and human again."

"I'm glad," said Bishou softly. "She deserves better than what she got."

"And bed is a nice place to talk," her brother concurred. "She's never had a regular man, and she's devoted to work." He looked down at Bishou. "She's older than I am. But man. She knows what she wants from me."

"And you gave it."

"Yeah. I did." Bat gazed into distant fields. "You know, when I first saw this house in daylight, I liked it. It reminded me of Nam. The best lady-houses were houses like this."

Bishou almost laughed. "You mean this house reminded you of the Southeast Asian bordellos?"

"Oui."

"I suppose it makes sense. French colonials started estates out there, too, and then went home and left their houses behind."

"Mm, oui. And the best madams bought the best houses. Of course, they're now kinda run-down, but at least they try to stay elegant. And they have to like you before they let you in." Bat blew out cigarette smoke. "They were dainty, tiny ladies, sometimes speaking a little French, not much."

This was a side of Bat's life she hadn't thought much about.

"Louis knows his stuff, doesn't he? About sex."

"Oui." She found it difficult even to speak to her brother about it. "He apologizes for being rough, but he's not, really. I can take it."

"I'm trying to be gentler with Adrienne, but hell. I lose control. And y'know? For all her prudishness and put-ons, she can handle me just fine."

"What're you going to do when you go back to America?"

"Not an issue. We've already agreed to have fun together while we can. We're all going up to Paris after this. The boys will have Celie's old bedroom, and I'll sleep with Adrienne. We're going sight-seeing."

"She's coming back from an exotic island trip with a sexy American boyfriend," Bishou smiled.

She could see Bat's white teeth in the dim light. "A little moral support, too. She took off like shit shot out of a cannon, and now she's going to have to see if she's still got a job."

"You're good at moral support, brother." Her arm was around his waist.

Bat smiled down at her. "So are you, little sister." He took a puff. "I was wondering if you'd admit the sexy part. Not about me, about you. After all, *nous sommes les jumeaux.*"

"We are the twins," she agreed.

"She knows you're faithful to Louis, and him to you. You're family. Me, she figures I have girlfriends all over the world, and now she's the one I visit when I come to Paris. She's got no problem with that. She's got a life of her own, too."

"So maybe this will all work out for the best," Bishou murmured.

"I think it might," Bat agreed.

They turned their heads at the sound of a man's voice, calling from the Dessants' bedroom.

"I think you've been missed," said Bat. He leaned over and kissed her. "Hey—thanks."

"Hey—thanks," she returned, and went back inside.

Louis was sitting up in bed, watching her as she closed the door. "Were you outside?" he asked quietly.

"*Non.* The birds woke me up, and Bat too. We were standing on the landing of the stairs."

"*Viens.*" As she came toward the bed, he said, "*Non.* Undress."

She obliged, removing her robe and setting it on the chair. He reached out for her as she climbed onto the bed. He was warm.

There was still a slight scent of men's cologne as he nuzzled her neck and wrapped his arms around her naked body. He sighed in her ear, "*Ma belle femme.*"

"Ah, *oui*," she sighed. Immediately, he slipped off his pajama bottoms and rolled her on her back. He slid atop her and made himself comfortable there.

He kissed her throat. "Ah, *oui.*"

The best madams had the best houses, Bat had said. And they had to like you before they let you in.

*

The white convertible followed the old gray Ford to the airport. Bat let his brothers and Adrienne off at the terminal. Bishou and Louis helped unload the luggage from the Ford's trunk. Then, Bat drove off to return his car to the rental area.

Etien and Denise Campard pulled up, too, to wish them farewell. They stood and waited for Bat to walk back to join them, and went inside to the Air France desk. Louis stepped over to the counter and bought the four tickets, while they waited on the sidelines. He returned, and gave Bat three tickets, Adrienne one. "The next flight leaves for Orly in half an hour," Louis told them. "We were just in time."

"I'll write when we get home," Bat told Bishou. "Maybe you'll get a postcard or two from Paris, though. I haven't really thought out how long we'll stay. But I'm starting to get worried about Dad and Maman."

"I know," said Bishou.

Bat put his arms around her, drew her close, and kissed her lovingly. "You've done some right things, but this is the rightest thing you've ever done, little sister. This is gonna be good."

"I think so, too. But I'll miss you all."

Louis was holding Gerry. They both had tears in their eyes.

"Little brother," Louis said to him, "never forget that this is your home, too." He also reached out and patted Andy's shoulder. Andy was trying to act too mature to cry, which was futile when every other member of the party was weeping.

As the boys said goodbye to the Campards, Louis reached out to Adrienne. She nestled in his arms, weeping too. "I am so glad you came," Louis told her. "I am so glad we could end this nightmare."

"*Aussi*," she sobbed quietly. "I will—I will return when I am a godmother. That I have promised Bishou."

Louis smiled through his tears. "*Bon*, we will see you then."

They saw them onto the plane. Louis's arm was wrapped about Bishou's shoulders, and Etien's around Denise's. They saw the boys wave goodbye. Then the plane taxied down the runway, and took off for the north.

Louis wiped his eyes and blew his nose. Then he looked down at his wife. "*Bien*, back to life as usual, *hein*?"

"I guess so," Bishou admitted. "Regular old married life."

Etien also blew his nose. "Who would ever have thought I would be sorry to see that harpy leave? But with you and Bat and the boys joking with her, she was a lot of fun."

"We have healed so many of the old wounds," said Louis. "You and I have worked very hard, *mon ami*, to come full circle. A beautiful wife for me. Happiness for you. The business intact. Living the lives we were meant to live."

"That's true." Etien, standing beside him, gazed off in the direction the airplane had taken. "I know you tell me never to worry. But this is the first time I feel I can take you at your word. I am going to go home, and—not worry for a change."

Chapter 15

Bishou entered the Arts & Humanities building, and the front office. "*Bon matin*, Mesdames!" she greeted the secretaries.

"*Bon matin*, Dr. Dessant!" they replied, equally cheerfully. Mme. Ellis came over to the counter.

"Well," said Bishou to her, "do I have an office, or even part of one? Or am I just here for a meeting?"

Mme. Ellis smiled. "You will be sharing an office with Dr. Castelle. Allow me to show you the way." She led Bishou down another corridor, to a door with a frosted glass panel. It was unlabeled.

Mme. Ellis tapped on the door. They heard, "*Entrez!*" She opened the door to show a small room, almost filled to capacity by two desks shoved against two bookcases, with a window off to one side.

Pierre Castelle turned to look at her. "Ah, Dr. Dessant! Welcome to our spacious suite."

"Thank you." Bishou turned to the secretary. "Thank you, Mme. Ellis."

"You'll need desk supplies—scissors, tape and so on," said the secretary. "Do drop back in a while to tell me what you need."

"Thank you. Let me get a little organized, first."

Mme. Ellis left, closing the door behind her.

Pierre Castelle said wryly, "I think this used to be the janitor's closet before it was willed to the least senior members."

Bishou smiled. "No, janitor's closets usually don't have windows."

"Good point. I will say, I have been in here by myself for a year, and I don't know how well I'm going to take to a roommate."

"We will adjust." Bishou set her bag and purse on the desk. "Can I make some suggestions?"

Pierre shrugged.

"If we put the bookcases along the back wall, and abut our desks in the middle, it will feel more spacious and will also give us wall space to hang pictures and our diplomas."

"Well thought." He stood. "All right, let's do it. I could use the exercise and the mental challenge."

They started shoving furniture around and hunting for outlets. Pierre emptied his bookshelves so that he could move them more easily. He grinned and admitted, "I feel like a freshman again."

"No, you're a second-year. I'm the freshman," Bishou laughed. "Here, let's turn the desks this way. You get the side with the window, you're senior member."

"La la la, it's good for something," he grinned.

Soon they had the furniture moved. Bishou helped him reload his bookcase.

"Don't you have books?" he asked.

"Not with me. They're still in America. I might ask someone to send my personal notes, but I don't know what else I will bother to ship."

Pierre stared at her in surprise. "You really came here cold, didn't you?"

"Mm, *oui*. I hadn't made any concrete plans to stay."

"*Merde de merde*. And now you're teaching freshman literature, and you're married."

"Come on, you've been a grad student. You know what it's like to be an academic nomad."

Pierre laughed, and looked at the walls. "No picture hooks, nothing. We don't even get our names on the door. At least it doesn't say 'Janitorial staff only.'"

Bishou opened the ancient metal desk that had been assigned to her, and slid a carton of Dessants in the drawer.

"What are those, cigarettes?" Pierre asked.

"*Non*, bribes." She pulled out her silver-framed photo of Louis and put on her desk.

"*Votre mari?*" Pierre asked with a grin.

"Yes. Are you married?"

"Not exactly. I live with a Parisian student who attended université with me."

"You don't have her photo out."

"We don't believe in that kind of thing. I hate to be rude, but it is rather bourgeois, isn't it?"

"Oh. Perhaps you're right. I could probably make up a convincing argument if I weren't so in love with the man I married."

Again, Pierre grinned. "I will provide a nice Paris travel poster for the wall."

"That sounds good." Bishou slid her purse into the drawer. Another drawer contained keys to the desk. "I presume our office door doesn't lock."

"It locks, but not well," Pierre said. "I had to jimmy the lock a couple of times when I forgot my keys."

Bishou put a box of Dessants in her pocket, then locked her desk. "When do we meet? I forgot."

"Eleven, in the Dean's office," Pierre replied.

"I will see you there, then, if not before." Bishou slid the cigarettes into her tote bag. "I want to wander around a bit."

"All right, *à toute à l'heure.*" Pierre sat at his desk again, and began reading the book he had placed there.

Bishou wandered down the hall, toward the back of the building. Eventually, she found what she wanted—the janitor, a Creole man easily in his forties. "*Bonjour, monsieur.*"

He regarded her curiously and cautiously. "*Bonjour*, Madame. What may I do for you?"

"Do you perform all the chores for this building? Because I

need a favor." She reached into her bag and pulled out four or five cigarettes.

He smiled, and held out his hand. Bishou dropped the cigarettes into his palm. "What do you need, Madame?"

She explained about the posters and picture frames they wanted to hang, and actually wrote down what she wanted painted on the glass door.

"I need to get special tools to put nails in the concrete, Dr. Dessant," said the janitor, whose name was Leon. "They might have some in one of the other buildings—let me go ask. And I'll do the painting tonight, after everyone has gone home—so the paint can dry."

"Small and neat," she reminded him. "We are the most junior teachers here. We don't want trouble."

"Small and neat," he promised. "It will be nice work. No other professor will be jealous."

Bishou thanked him, then went back to see the secretaries. They provided her with a pad of paper, some envelopes, a desk blotter, paper clips, a few pens, and some tape. She carried them back to the office.

Pierre looked up from his book. "It's about that time."

"Where do we meet?"

"In the conference room just off the Dean's office."

Pierre led the way down the hall, through the secretaries' domain, to a second door next to the Dean's office. Other men were already gathered at the big table there. It looked more like they were getting ready for a round of poker than for an academic discussion. "Ah, Dr. Dessant," Dr. Rubin greeted her. "I see you are finding your way about."

"Merci. I have a good guide in Dr. Castelle," she replied, pulling up a seat to the table.

"I haven't shown her the faculty lounge yet," said Pierre with a grin, "because I fear they will expect the woman to make coffee every morning—and I fear her response."

Dr. Rubin actually chuckled. "That will be your next hurdle, Dr. Dessant. Right now, though—let's discuss the schedule."

He might as well have said, "Let's deal." Dr. Rubin had little index cards, which he dealt to various professors when they volunteered to teach certain courses, and they all kept lists of who had agreed to what. Mme. Ellis, the secretary, sat at one side and took notes. Seven or eight o'clock was not considered an unreasonable hour here, since the University, too, honored the afternoon siesta, everywhere called the "closure," from noon to two. Some classes started at seven in the morning—not an issue for Bishou, who avoided late courses, since she had a husband to go home to, and Pierre had expressed a preference for afternoon and evening time slots.

As expected, she ended up with the Introduction to World Literature sections. However, since they had a large number of university applicants this year, and Dr. Rubin had just managed to have a graduation requirement of at least one Literature course accepted by the university, there were four sections. Bishou volunteered for them all, and then jockeyed for time slots. She ended up with two Monday-Wednesday sections, an early Tuesday-Thursday section, and one Wednesday-Friday section, and was satisfied.

Pierre Castelle stared at her. "Mon Dieu, the same thing four times. I'd lose my mind. Makes me glad I'm keeping the Writing Lab open—I was almost tempted to offer it to you."

"The sections are not exactly the same thing," Bishou said defensively. "It depends on the type of student in the class. It won't take me long to find out which are the drama and lit students, which are the science majors, and which are the jocks, and adjust accordingly."

"What about textbooks?" asked Dr. Rubin.

"My sister-in-law at the Bibliothèque Nationale de France tells me that Yohannan's *Treasury of Asian Literature* has been translated into French. It's available as a paperback, and not very expensive. I can use that for readings, or at least as guidelines, for the Eastern literature. I may find a similar sampler of Western literature, or I may end up putting some books on reserve at the library."

"I want to see some ethics and philosophy woven into that, too," said the Dean. "Do you feel up to it?"

"Of course I do, or I wouldn't have offered," Bishou replied.

"*Merde!*" said Dr. Robert, "you have taken on a gigantic task."

"There's more to it than that," Bishou replied seriously. "I want them to think about perhaps becoming lit majors, too."

Some of the other professors looked disbelieving, but Dr. Rubin sat back, satisfied. "You've struck off my meaning exactly, Dr. Dessant. That is why I have worked so hard to make Introduction to World Literature a required course. These students must have some acquaintance with true scholarship, and this may be the only chance we get at them, before they go off into sports coaching or organic chemistry or nursing or pre-law or pre-med, or whatever. You don't get scholarship off the football field."

"Or perhaps you do," she said seriously. "That's where the true sportsmen come from, but there's only one or two of those per generation."

Pierre Castelle joked, "I don't think I'm up to breathing this rarefied air of academia."

"You're the best example of the philosophy," Bishou told him.

He blinked. "*Pardon? Quoi? Moi?*"

"You were in the student riots, weren't you?"

"Well, yes, I was."

"Why were you protesting?"

"We had wretched conditions—"

Bishou interrupted him, very civilly. "No, I didn't ask you *what* you were protesting. I asked *why*."

Thoughtfully, he replied, "Because it seemed like the right

thing to do. All right, I get your point. Do you think that will prevent equally violent riots here?"

"I don't know. But students are more likely to work within the system if they feel the administration is open to communication, don't you think? And Paris certainly has its hands full."

The other professors looked thoughtful, too. Dr. Rubin, however, looked vindicated. "All right, Dr. Dessant, you've got openers. Can you work in some information on how to study and how to delegate time to homework?"

"That's part of it," she agreed.

"*Bon.* This will leave the gentlemen free for some other necessary courses, so it would be nice if I have you in the fundamentals. I want a Modern Réunionnais Literature course this semester— Theo, see if you can get Gamaleya as a guest speaker, or other *réunionnais* authors—free if they'll come to your class, if they want an evening on stage, we'll start looking for sources of honoraria."

Theo duVerger almost dived for his notebook. "Wonderful."

"We need to break down Literature of the Middle Ages—I want Literature of the Capetian Dynasty, Literature of the Valois and Orleans Dynasties, Literature of the 16th and 17th Centuries, Literature of the 18th Century, on into the Republics."

"Can't some of that wait until the next semester?" Pierre objected. "We should be doing some Moderns, too, and that's going to fill all our schedules with old stuff."

"We need to do some individual authors, as well," Dukette objected.

"All right," said the Dean. "Pick your topics, then."

It really is like a card game, Bishou thought. The professors happily chose what they would teach this term, under the guidance of the Dean. Out popped Literature of the 1950s, American Literature, Canadian Literature, Modern French Fiction, Modern French Poetry, Heritage of Jewish Literature, as well as Peguy, Cocteau, Saint-Exupery, Maupassant, Maeterlinck, Voltaire,

Anouilh, Hugo, Dumas. They shuffled them all into a working schedule as best they could, and threw the rest of their cards back in the deck for the next hand.

"What will the History Department do this semester?" Dr. Weis asked.

"Consult us," Rubin chuckled. He started dealing cards. "Now, these are your new advisees. You'll see them each, at least once. I know some of you like group meetings, some of you prefer individual ones. The choice is yours. Just log in the meetings, please, so they appear on the students' records. Then, if something happens, we're documented. Dr. Dessant. Is this your first time as an advisor?"

"*Non, Monsieur le Doyen.* I advised undergraduates when I was a graduate assistant and tutor at East Virginia University."

"*Bon.* But you will report back to me on each advisory session, at least for this first semester, in writing or in person, before I give you a free hand. You are still on probation."

"*Oui, Monsieur le Doyen.*"

"Here are academic calendars for all of you. I must emphasize that Convocation is a week from Wednesday, at 7:00 p.m. as all students should be arriving or registering that day. That means be here, in the lobby of this building, at 6:45 for the processional, in full academicals. Do you have yours, Dr. Dessant?"

"*Oui, Monsieur le Doyen.*"

He eyed Pierre. "And you, Dr. Castelle? With no plaid or print shirt visible, I hasten to add."

Pierre grinned. "*Oui, Monsieur le Doyen.*"

"Very well. Convocation, and the opening reception after, and the academic year officially starts. Be there. I *will* take attendance." Then he dismissed them, and rose to return to his own office.

As they left the meeting, Bishou murmured to Pierre, "I see why you like it here."

Pierre Castelle nodded. "Everything is a blank slate. It's all new.

Dr. Rubin is from the Sorbonne. You'd expect him to be a hide-bound and conservative Dean, and he's not. He is tremendously innovative. He's always pushing where it gives. He's nothing like one expects. When I come out of these meetings, I feel like I've been at a sports rally."

Bishou laughed quietly. "I feel the same way." She glanced toward the front lobby, and saw a familiar figure. She touched Pierre's arm. "Stay a moment."

The lobby windows silhouetted the man as he peered down the corridor, and walked toward them uncertainly. Of course, the corridor appeared dark to him, since the light was behind him. He could not see them well.

"Louis," said Bishou.

The man stopped for a moment, then walked toward them with more confidence. It was, indeed, Louis. He came up to her and smiled. "It's lunchtime. I came to take you home."

"*Bon*. Our meeting just finished. *Mon cher*, allow me to introduce Dr. Pierre Castelle, who shares an office with me. Pierre, my husband, Louis Dessant."

The men shook hands. "I remember you," said Louis, "from the lecture. It is good to meet you again."

"*Aussi*," said Pierre. "Care to come admire our coat-closet?"

Bishou laughed, and walked with the men to the tiny office. Pierre opened the door. They stepped inside.

"Well, at least three can stand inside the door," said Louis.

"True," Bishou agreed, "now that we have re-arranged it."

"*Regardez!*" Pierre pointed. There were now hangers neatly inserted in portions of the cement wall. "Spaces for the Paris poster and for our diplomas! The janitor has been busy. Those bribes are working, Dr. Dessant!"

Louis chuckled. "Carton of cigarettes in the bottom drawer, eh?"

"But of course," said Pierre. "And now we have picture hooks."

Louis was already staring at the desks and saw his own photograph on one, but he said nothing.

Out in the car, Louis said, "I never expected to see my picture on an office desk."

"I'm sorry. Does it offend you?"

"No. It merely feels—strange to me. My wife," he mused, "has her husband's picture on her desk at work. Such an ordinary thing."

Bishou leaned over and kissed him. "It's the next best thing to having you there."

"What did Pierre mean about seeing you Wednesday night?"

"There is a university ceremony next week Wednesday. Convocation. The start of the new academic year."

"It's September."

"That's when an academic year starts," Bishou replied. "Our guest speaker will be the university Chancellor. All faculty will be in attendance, in full academicals."

"Meaning?"

"I will wear my doctoral gown, which you bought for me and have not yet seen."

Louis started up the car, and pulled out of the space before he smiled at her. "Oh, it will be worth it just for that. Or may outsiders attend this?"

"Outsiders may attend this, but you are not an outsider. You are a faculty spouse."

Louis glanced at her. "This is new territory for both of us, isn't it? You as a professor and me as a professor's spouse."

"Yes, it is. We might need to tread carefully for a while, until we learn our places in all this."

"If you could do it in East Virginia University, I can do it here," Louis replied. "I will try not to embarrass you."

"You won't," she said. "If anything, I might embarrass you."

"*Nous verrons.*" We'll see.

Chapter 16

"You would think we didn't own a couch," Denise chided, as she brought coffee over to the Dessants, seated on her rug. She gave Etien his cup, and sat in a chair near Louis and Bishou.

"We can cuddle better this way." Louis wrapped his arms around his wife. "Besides, it's a nice rug."

"So you are now an official university professor," Etien said, sipping his coffee. "Teaching classes, and everything." Unlike Louis, he had attended university.

"Are you coming to Convocation next Wednesday?" Bishou asked them.

"That's the official opening of the academic year, isn't it?" Denise asked. "Mme. Cantrell was saying something about attending."

"I will be there," said Louis, "a thorn in a field of roses."

"Or vice versa," said his wife, with a sly look, and he grinned.

"Do you have a teaching schedule yet?" Etien asked Bishou.

"I do, and it's a rough one," Bishou replied. "Not just because I'm a beginning teacher. This is the largest freshman class they've ever admitted, over a thousand students, and I'm the only lecturer in their only required Arts and Humanities course."

"*Merde de merde!* A thousand students!" Etien exclaimed. "No wonder they were happy to get your application."

"*Bien dit,*" Bishou agreed. "I teach just the sort of thing they need, and I have a voice that can reach a lecture hall of 300 students. They're supposed to get me a grad assistant, but I'll believe that when I see it. I think I'm in this all alone."

"Including quizzes and examinations?" Etien stared.

"I think *Monsieur le Doyen* will help me out on those, since I'm technically on probation. But I've got something at 0800 every day of the week. On Monday and Wednesday, I'll be going until 1530 heures, but the other days, I'll be done by noon. Thank goodness."

"You'll still come over on Friday nights, then," said Denise.

Bishou and Louis looked at each other, and smiled. "That was non-negotiable," said Louis. "We have discussed this."

"And included Bettina and Madeleine in the discussions," Bishou added.

"Friday nights, we are here. If we invite guests over to our home, we will try to do it on Wednesday nights. More likely, people who invite us to their homes tend to do so on Saturday nights."

"That's when the Prefect and his wife tend to hold dinners, and we are obliged," said Bishou.

"Mm, *oui*," her husband agreed. "But there are enough people—you know, Etien, salesmen and their wives from work, and Bishou's new office-mate and his girlfriend, and others—that we want to be able to invite over for dinner some time."

"A normal life," Etien murmured. Then he asked, "So how big is the staff, to advise a thousand students?"

"Oh, they're not all Arts & Humanities. It's not as daunting as it looks at first glance."

"But surely, with as much work as you're doing, it's not part-time, as you planned," said Etien.

"Well," Bishou admitted uncomfortably, "no. I've got a full academic load, but that's only for now. We're going to take it one semester at a time."

"Then you aren't getting benefits you are entitled to, as a full-time employee." Etien frowned.

"Pfah," said Louis.

"Pfah, my sugar daddy," she agreed, kissing his cheek. "And it means that I can take a semester off with no courses, because it averages out as part-time, do you see?"

"Why would you want to take a semester off?" asked Etien.

However, Denise smiled to herself and drank coffee.

"Oh, I don't know," Bishou replied easily. "Perhaps I would take some time off and travel around this beautiful island. Perhaps I would write a textbook. Perhaps I would volunteer somewhere."

"Perhaps you might have a child," Louis suggested, in a soft voice.

Bishou smiled into his eyes. "Having a child! What an idea!"

Louis's eyes and smile were as gentle as his voice had been. "One never knows."

"Well," Etien prodded, "are you?"

Bishou blinked at him. "Am I what?"

"*Enciente.*"

"Even if I was, Etien Campard," said Bishou, "do you think you would be the first person I told?"

Denise giggled. "Especially if we're going to a special occasion where nothing must be said about it."

"I am not a good liar," Etien said, "so I'm lucky you aren't pregnant, so I won't have to attempt to lie."

"That's the spirit," said Bishou.

Gently, Louis kissed her cheek. He did not appear confused, shocked, or stunned. He wrapped his arms around her. Etien and Denise smiled down at them.

*

In the car, in the dark, on the way home, Louis said, "You are, aren't you?"

"I was pretty certain you knew all along," Bishou replied.

"I thought about why you called me Papa." His hand rubbed her thigh. "You wanted me to father a child."

"Not *a* child, Louis. *Your* child."

"For how long have you been *enceinte*?"

"Since the beginning."

"Since the beginning," he mused, rubbing her thigh again while he drove. "And yet you planned all this, the university and your teaching."

"*Oui*, I did."

"Why? Just so you would not be a burden to me, another parasite?"

"That, and also, to justify the time and money I have spent on my education, and to honor my promises to my family."

"To Bat, you mean."

"*Oui*, to Bat."

"And you have not broken your promises to him."

"*Non.*"

"To whom else have you made promises?"

"To you, *mon treasor.*"

They pulled up in front of the house. "Any other promises?"

"No, only the one to love and cherish *mon mari* all my life. Just that one."

Louis did not move to get out of the car. It took Bishou a moment to realize why. She felt for her purse, pulled out her handkerchief, and wiped tears from his face. He stopped her hand. His voice was very quiet and calm. "*Non, ma Bishou*, don't bother. I am just—enjoying the feeling—that I could die happy at this moment."

"I sincerely hope not, Papa. There are many more years for us."

"*Oui.* But they will be years of—caring for our children, commuting to work, trading letters and telephone calls with friends and family, even—even growing old together. Those ordinary pleasures that I thought were forever denied me." He leaned over. Those soft lips touched hers. "Thank you."

"Non, *mon cheri*. Thank you. For reaching out and welcoming me."

ABOUT THE AUTHOR

Linda Kepner is a genre fiction author living in New Hampshire, and employed at America's oldest public library. Her other books include *Second Chance,* the previous volume of Bishou's story. Linda has worked as a librarian, college instructor, magazine editor, and brokerage clerk. *Second Chance Sister* is her fourth novel. For more information about the author, please see her web site: *www.lindatkepner.com.*

In the mood for more Crimson Romance? Check out *The Abolitionist's Secret* by Becky Lower at CrimsonRomance.com.

www.ingramcontent.com/pod-product-compliance
Lightning Source LLC
Chambersburg PA
CBHW010640100726
47900CB00011B/2906